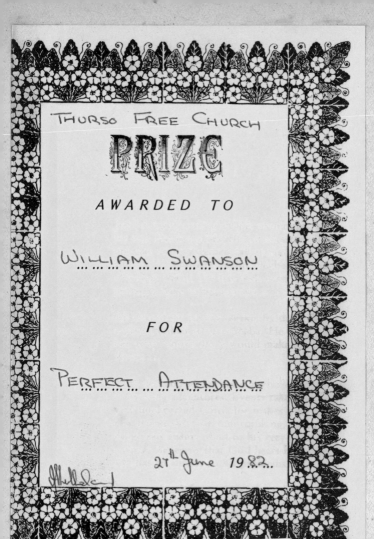

THURSO FREE CHURCH

PRIZE

AWARDED TO

WILLIAM SWANSON

FOR

PERFECT ATTENDANCE

27th June 1982

TO MY TWO CHILDREN, PETER AND LINDSAY

KILLER DOG

Peggy Burns

A LION PAPERBACK

Copyright © 1981 Peggy Burns

Published by
Lion Publishing
Icknield Way, Tring, Herts, England
ISBN 0 85648 383 4
Albatross Books
PO Box 320, Sutherland, NSW 2232, Australia
ISBN 0 86760 319 4

First edition 1981

Illustrations by David Astin

Typeset by V & M Graphics Ltd,
Aylesbury, Bucks
Printed and bound in Great Britain
by Richard Clay (The Chaucer Press) Ltd,
Bungay, Suffolk

Contents

1 The nightmare begins   7
2 An exhausting journey   15
3 Unwanted company   23
4 Joe in danger   30
5 First aid and grasshoppers   37
6 Awkward questions   44
7 The watcher on the cliff   52
8 Where is Sheba?   60
9 Steve and Liz stick their necks out   70
10 Joe makes up his mind ...   76
11 ... and finds out for himself   84

CHAPTER 1

THE NIGHTMARE BEGINS

The Radcliffe Hall school bus was crowded with noisy, laughing – and sometimes quarrelling – boys. Joe, sitting in a corner by himself, was in a dream world of his own. He was reliving the afternoon session at the school's swimming-pool; his moment of triumph, when Mr Gordon, the swimming coach, had timed him yet again with the stop-watch.

'Not bad,' he had told the enthusiastic Joe. 'Not bad at all, Brooke! A whole five seconds' improvement on the last time,' and Joe had glowed with pride, knowing well how rarely Mr Gordon ever praised a boy. Joe knew that his 'not bad' really meant 'jolly good'. After the period, Mr Gordon had taken Joe aside.

'When the Spring holiday's over, I'll be training a team of boys to swim for the school,' he had said. 'Like to join it, Brooke? I think you can make it.'

Would he like to! Joe was exultant. He had two passions in life: swimming, and his dog Sheba. Three passions really, thought the sports-mad Joe, if you counted football in winter. And next season, he might even make the school team. But for now, he would concentrate on his swimming.

Already the inhabitants of the village of Heystock were used to seeing Joe, each evening after his homework was finished, clad in a royal blue

7

tracksuit, jogging around the recreation ground as part of his training programme. And always with him ran his dog Sheba, a beautiful Irish setter, her satiny coat glowing red-gold, her delicately feathered tail waving excitedly in the sheer joy of living.

It was no wonder Joe was keen on sport. He was tall for his age, strong and sturdy, yet without an ounce of spare flesh. His long legs and unruly mop of dark hair were always to be seen in the thick of any game.

Joe almost missed his stop. Mr Stiggs, the driver, honked impatiently as he waited. Joe was the only boy who got out at Heystock.

Unheeding, Joe stared blissfully into space. In imagination, he had just broken his own record and beaten David Gill, the champion swimmer at their rival school, winning the cup for Radcliffe Hall. His pleasant daydream came to an abrupt end.

'Wake up, Joe,' a boy shouted in his ear.

Joe came down to earth with a bump, and hurriedly shouldered his bag of books. Mr Stiggs hooted again, long and hard, startling two elderly ladies on the pavement.

'Let me know when you decide whether to get off or not,' he said to Joe, sarcastically.

Joe's ears went rather pink as he hurried down the gangway, but he said nothing. He jumped from the bus to a chorus of cheers, and turned to wave lightheartedly to his friends. He watched as the driver revved his engine noisily, grated the gears, and drew away suddenly, jerking his passengers roughly, as always. Joe gave a thumbs-up sign to two boys who grinned at him from the rear window, chuckling briefly at the roughness of Mr Stiggs's driving, and began to whistle tunelessly as he turned down Acacia Avenue.

Pleasant visions of swimming trophies were

driven completely from his mind as he saw, parked outside his own house, a white police car. He was vaguely troubled as his mind ran swiftly over his recent escapades. But he could think of nothing which could possibly deserve a visit from the police. Even so, he was mildly relieved when he saw two uniformed officers leave the house and drive away.

Joe's father looked worried. Even Joe, as he slammed the front door behind him, could see that.

'What did the police want, Dad?' Joe demanded, flinging down his anorak and bag.

'Hang your coat up, Joe,' his mother said automatically, coming in from the kitchen with a pile of plates and cutlery, and beginning to lay the table for the evening meal. Joe sighed heavily, but did as he was told. He never could seem to remember to do things like hanging up coats and folding clothes.

'What did they want?' Joe asked his father again. 'I hope I'm not in any trouble ... If it's about that pane of glass in Mr Johnson's greenhouse, it wasn't me.'

'It's not that,' said his father seriously. 'Come and sit down, Joe.'

Feeling rather as if he were in the dentist's waiting-room, with a couple of teeth that needed filling, Joe sat down on the well-worn arm of the couch, and waited for his father to go on.

'The police were here about Sheba,' he told Joe after a pause.

'About Sheba?' Joe said, puzzled. He looked around for his dog. 'Where is Sheba?'

'She's chained up in the yard,' his father said grimly, and added, 'The police say she's been killing sheep up on High Fall.'

Joe was stunned.

'She can't have been,' he said. 'Sheba wouldn't

do a thing like that – I'll never believe it. It must have been some other dog.'

His father shook his head.

'I'd like to think it wasn't Sheba, Joe,' he said, 'but the police are positive about it.' He sighed. 'I know how much that dog means to you, but look at it from Mr Benson's point of view. He lost five sheep this week. Two of them were killed outright over the weekend, and a third one was so badly mauled, he had to have it put down this morning.'

'But Dad ...' Joe broke in, but his father held up his hand and went on.

'A couple of the farm workers saw the dog leaving – a red setter – and recognized it. It was Sheba. She *was* out late last night, you know.'

Joe did know, and was silent.

'What will happen now?' he said at last. 'Will we have to keep Sheba chained up all the time?'

A look passed between his parents, and then his mother looked away. His father cleared his throat and took off his glasses suddenly to rub at the lenses with a handkerchief.

'It's not as simple as that, son,' he said. 'Killing sheep is a very serious offence. One of those officers explained it all to us. What it boils down to is that we have to go to court. Then they'll weigh all the evidence and decide what's to be done with Sheba.'

'Can't we just promise to keep her in the yard, and only take her out on the lead?' interrupted Joe. 'We could easily do that.'

'There seems to be a lot of evidence against her,' said Joe's father. 'It's not the first time this has happened, nor the second either. Poor old Jim Benson's out of his mind with worry – always the same dog, he says. His men have caught sight of it before, but never had the chance of a shot at it. And Joe – you know as well as I do that Sheba's taken to

10

slipping out late in the evenings. That's bound to tell against her.'

Joe took a deep breath, but couldn't keep the tremble out of his voice.

'What do you think will happen, then?' he asked.

Joe's mother turned suddenly and went into the kitchen. Joe stared after her.

'Your Mum's upset,' his father said. 'I might as well tell you now as later, Joe, that things look bad for Sheba. That's what the police officers said – and it will probably end in us having to have Sheba put down.'

Joe suddenly felt sick. Have Sheba put down? Kill his dog? Sheba was more than just a dog to Joe. She was a friend. How could his father let this happen?

As if he knew what Joe was thinking, his father said, 'It's the law, son. It's very quick – they won't hurt her at all. And we must hope for the best – it might not come to that in the end.' He reached across and squeezed Joe's shoulder. 'I know how you must feel, son,' he said.

Abruptly, Joe left the room. He knew he would break down and cry like a girl if he talked any more. Sheba needed him now, he felt, and he went out to her, and buried his face in her glossy red coat.

✳   ✳   ✳

There was no sleep for Joe that night. Until long after his parents had gone to bed, he tossed and turned, reaching out from time to time to stroke Sheba's head and receive a worried lick from her. She knew something was troubling her beloved Joe, and comforted him in the only way she knew.

Joe remembered the day his father had brought Sheba home for him, a squirming, wriggling pup,

11

chewing rugs and making little puddles in the hallway – and the memory hurt.

'Hope for the best,' his father had said, 'it might not come to that.' But would it? The police had seemed pretty sure about it. And Dad had, too. They didn't give a lot for Sheba's chances. Suddenly, Joe knew that he couldn't just hang around, hoping for the best, but being sure that Sheba would have to be destroyed in the end. He had to save her, somehow. He had to make some plans.

'I don't believe you're a sheep killer, anyway, old girl,' Joe told her, fondling her long ears.

Sitting up in bed, Joe turned on the reading-lamp by his bed. It was a quarter past three, and already not quite as dark as it had been. He must take Sheba away. Right now, while it was still night. He would hitch a lift and take her far away, somewhere she would be quite safe. But where? Joe swung his legs out of bed and began to dress swiftly and silently. Plans crowded in on his mind now.

He remembered a long-ago visit to the seaside when he and his cousin Tim had found a cave along the rocky shore. What was the name of that place? Yes, Kestle Rocks. It was miles from anywhere. He and Sheba could stay there as long as they liked, in the cave. It was about forty miles south of his home. Hurry, hurry.

Fortunately, all the camping gear was stored in the boxroom. Joe tiptoed softly across the landing, past the closed door of his parents' room. One false step now, and it would all be over! Once inside the room he closed the door before turning on the light. He had never realised before how loud the click from a light-switch could sound in the silence of the night! Joe held his breath for a long time, wondering if his parents had heard it, but all was still. He relaxed.

12

Now, what would he need? Joe was faced with a bewildering array of camping equipment, all of which would need a large car to transport. He was strictly limited to what he could carry. His sleeping-bag. He would certainly need that. Even in June the nights could be very cool. Good, it was already neatly rolled up and securely tied. Into a rucksack he pushed a torch, a handful of cutlery and a plastic mug. All the other things he would have to do without.

He searched among his father's maps on a bookshelf until he found one showing the part of the coast around Kestle Rocks. That would be bound to come in useful.

When Joe tiptoed back to his own room, he left the boxroom light on, remembering the loud switch. His mother would turn it off in the morning. In the morning! Where would he be by then? From his drawer he took socks, underclothes and a thick jersey, crammed them into the rucksack, and slung it over his shoulder. Then, holding tightly to Sheba's collar, the sleeping-bag tucked awkwardly beneath his arm, he made his way downstairs to the kitchen.

Now to the problem of food. He couldn't take many tins of food because of the weight. But he crammed into the rucksack a few tins of Sheba's meat, some baked beans, a cake, biscuits and half a loaf of bread. A spare tin-opener and two boxes of matches joined them, and Joe thought he was ready.

As an afterthought, he raided his money-box and pushed all the money deep into his jeans' pocket. On his way through the hall, Joe grabbed his anorak, then jumped, startled, as the big grandfather clock unexpectedly began to strike the hour. Four o'clock. Not bad going, Joe thought, letting himself out by the back door.

13

Keeping strictly to the back streets, Joe and Sheba began to make their way towards the big main road, which by-passed Heystock about a mile away across the fields. Suddenly, a car swung into the lane, headlights full on. In panic, Joe pressed himself back into someone's open gateway. Had the driver seen him? The car passed without stopping. Joe, with wildly beating heart, heaved a sigh of relief, clipped a lead on to Sheba's collar, and the two crossed the lane, climbed a stile, and struck out across country.

It was very lonely, crossing the fields in the half-light, and Joe was glad of Sheba's company. He had been this way many times before in the daylight, but the deep shadows, moving threateningly with each breath of breeze, made everything eerie and strange. That one mile had never seemed as long before.

At last, though, this first lap of his journey was over, and he reached the main road, which was almost deserted at this time of the morning. Joe and Sheba crossed over and began to walk in the right direction, Joe holding out his thumb hopefully to each occasional lorry which thundered by. After what seemed like a long time, a large delivery van pulled up. Joe threw his sleeping-bag and rucksack into the cab, and thankfully climbed up after them.

CHAPTER 2

AN EXHAUSTING
JOURNEY

The driver of the van was a friendly northerner, and was obviously glad to have someone to talk to. A friendly chat was the last thing Joe felt like just then, but he pulled himself together and tried his best. He didn't want to make the driver suspicious! He told himself he was a boy just setting out for a holiday, and tried to act like one. But he hadn't bargained for the driver's curiosity.

'Where are you off to, then, so early in the morning?' he wanted to know.

'I'm going to spend a week with my aunt in the country,' Joe told him. 'My Mum hasn't been well lately, so she'll be able to have a rest,' he added, inventing rapidly. Joe was usually a truthful boy, but he could make up stories by the dozen if the occasion called for it.

'Getting rid of you for a bit, eh?' said the driver, changing gear at the foot of a hill. He pulled out to overtake a labouring lorry which was making heavy weather of the incline. Joe nodded.

'Are there a lot of you at home, then?' asked his chatty new friend. Joe wondered briefly whether to invent half a dozen brothers and sisters, but decided that would only complicate things.

'No, there's only me, and my dog, of course,' said Joe.

'Won't your aunt mind you taking him with you? He looks as though he could get through a lot of grub.'

'She,' said Joe. 'It's a she. And my aunt likes dogs.'

'I'm rather partial to cats myself,' said the driver. 'I've three of them at home. Not that dogs aren't good company, too,' he added hastily, not wanting to offend Joe.

Joe was finding the conversation hard going, so he let his eyelids close and pretended to be nodding off to sleep. Before long, the feigned sleep became real, and Joe dozed fitfully.

He awoke to find himself being prodded in the ribs. The morning sun, now well risen, shone straight into his eyes.

'This is where I turn off,' the driver said. 'Which way are you going?'

'I'm making for the London road,' said Joe untruthfully, rubbing the sleep from his eyes. 'That passes quite near to where my aunt lives.'

'Well, if you wait in the lay-by further along this road, you should get another lift soon enough,' said the good-natured driver. 'Have a good time at your aunt's!'

'I will – and thanks for the lift,' said Joe, slamming the door of the cab. The driver lifted his hand in a brief salute as the van drew away. Joe and Sheba were alone again.

Joe glanced at his watch. He was surprised to see that it was only just after six. His parents would not be up until 7.30. He could count on an hour and a half before the alarm was raised and people started to look for him. He looked around, not recognizing the place at all. Behind him were fields. Across the road was a run-down transport café and filling-station, advertising itself – rather shabbily – as the

'Paradise Snack Bar'. Joe, feeling very empty now, wondered whether he should buy himself some breakfast before he went on. He hesitated, knowing that the police would be bound to trace him to the café. A boy and a dog travelling alone so early in the day would be remembered easily. Then he realised that they would find out anyway, sooner or later, where the van driver had dropped him off. Hunger at last made Joe's mind up for him.

Early morning traffic was building up now, and there were a lot more lorries and cars about. Joe led Sheba across the busy road and into the transport café. The only other customer was a young lorry driver who sprawled in a corner reading last night's newspaper.

A plump woman in a blue overall was energetically wiping down table tops with a dishcloth. She looked up disapprovingly as Joe and Sheba came in.

'No dogs allowed,' she said sharply. 'Can't you read?'

Joe had not seen the notice on the swing door. It said 'No dogs, in the interests of hygiene'. He led Sheba outside again, and tied her lead to a wire litter bin.

The woman was filling sugar basins as Joe went back inside, and he waited impatiently as she finished her jobs. At last, she gave the top of the glass display unit a rub with the dishcloth, squeezed through a narrow gap in the counter, and with expert aim tossed the cloth into a sink in the corner.

'What do you want then?' she asked Joe, drying her hands carefully on a rough towel.

'A cup of tea, please, and a ham sandwich,' said Joe, wishing he could afford some of the bacon and eggs he could smell, frying in the kitchen at the back.

'Come a long way?' the woman asked him,

thawing a little as she filled a pint pot with very strong tea.

'Mmm ...' said Joe, noncommitally. He wondered if people always asked so many questions, or whether it just seemed that they did, because he didn't want to answer them.

'You're out very early,' she said, cutting Joe a very generous 'doorstep' sandwich. 'Got far to go?'

Joe stuck to the story he had told the van driver. 'I'm going to my aunt's,' he said. 'She lives on the London road.'

'That'll be a nice change for you,' the woman said chattily. 'Hitch-hiking, I suppose?'

As Joe paid for his breakfast, she filled a bowl with fresh water and pushed it across the counter.

'That's for your dog,' she said. 'He's probably thirsty, travelling.'

Evidently his new friend's bark was worse than her bite, thought Joe as he carried the bowl outside to Sheba, who began to lap gratefully. He took his own meal to a corner of the café, and spread his map across the table as he ate. He needed to know where he was.

It was easy to find the crossroads where the café was. Not far down the road was the village of Byford Green – that was where he turned off. He reckoned he had another five miles or so to go to reach the sea. It would be safer to walk the rest of the way, rather than get another lift. He hoped the police would think that he'd gone on towards London.

Between the café and the coast was a wooded area. Joe hoped that by keeping to the trees he could reach the sea without meeting anyone. After all, it was still very early. Not many people were about at this hour.

Before he left the café, Joe bought himself a large bottle of lemonade. He might not find fresh water

18

straight away. He looked in dismay at his money. It wasn't going to last very long if he spent it at this rate. From now on he must buy as little as he could.

Sheba jumped up gladly with waving tail to welcome Joe as he came out of the café. He made a fuss of her, and she licked the boy's face affectionately. Joe was more determined than ever to save her life. How could a dog as lovable as Sheba ever turn to killing sheep for a pastime?

Joe forked right at the crossroads. The road wound through the tiny village, and there was very little traffic about. Bedroom curtains were still closed, and Joe met nobody on the road. Still, he felt very uneasy until he reached the narrow country lane he was looking for. A signpost read 'Public footpath to Kelwith Cove – 4 miles'. Joe knew from the map that Kelwith Cove was just around the bay from Kestle Rocks.

Thankfully, he led Sheba up the pleasant little lane and away from the houses. The morning sun filtered through the leaves of trees whose branches arched above him. Joe heard the birds all the time when he was at home, but here, in this quiet country place, he could really say that they *sang*.

If he had not been in such a desperate hurry, Joe would really have enjoyed this walk. Sheba was enjoying it. She badly wanted to be let off the lead. But Joe hurried her on as fast as he could. Time was running out. In a matter of minutes now, his parents would find out that he was missing, 'phone the police, and then the hunt would be on.

Four miles through the woods and across fields seemed a very long way to the weary Joe. He was almost ready to give up when he smelled it – that unmistakable seaweedy, salty smell of the sea. Joe's heart gave a glad leap, and new life seemed to flow into his tired feet. It couldn't be far now!

19

Then, as Joe reached the edge of the wood, he saw the sea – a deep blue and sparkling in the sun. Here the lane began to curve inland again, but a stile took Joe and Sheba over the wall and into an overgrown path through deep sand dunes.

Another ten minutes' hard walking took Joe to the deserted sandy beach which was Kelwith Cove. Kestle Rocks were to the west – further than Joe would have thought. But at last he reached his goal. The soft, grassy dunes had given way to rougher walking, with rocks and boulders strewn across the shingly beach.

The hills became higher until they towered, true cliffs, above the sea. This was a desolate spot, far off the beaten track. The cliffs were the haunt of sea-birds which cried dismally as they rode on the wind and skimmed the white tips of the waves, stirring memories and recalling to Joe's mind that unforgettable holiday.

Long ago, when Joe had been very small, his family had visited this very spot, and he and his cousin had wandered off by themselves. While exploring, they had found the cave and played in it all afternoon. Joe still remembered the trouble they had been in when they got back to their frantic families, who were almost ready to send out search parties for the missing boys.

Where was that cave, now? It couldn't be far away. Joe began to search again for it. Then he saw it – well-hidden among the rocks, yet just by another stretch of sandy beach.

The cave was much smaller than Joe remembered, though it went a long way back into the cliff. Then he realised that it wasn't the cave that had shrunk, but he who'd grown bigger! Still, it was big enough. And what a fantastic hiding-place! After his nerve-racking journey, it was like coming home.

As weary as Joe felt, he could not rest until he had looked after Sheba. He had had some breakfast, but Sheba had only had a bowl of water. Joe opened a tin of meat for her and scraped the food out on to a flat stone. As she ate hungrily, Joe gave in to his weariness. Curling up on the sandy floor of the cave, he sank into a deep, exhausted sleep.

CHAPTER 3

UNWANTED COMPANY

Joe's sleep did not refresh him. He woke a few hours later, stiff and sore. The sand which had seemed so soft at first, now felt as hard as concrete. That was the first thing he had to do, thought Joe, as he rubbed an aching hip-bone – gather armfuls of grass and leaves to make a softer bed!

Worse than his aches and pains, though, was the feeling inside him, which Joe couldn't put a name to; an awful, leaden feeling in the pit of his stomach – the worry, fear and guilt of the past night, all mixed up together.

The excitement which had kept him going until he reached the cave had now ebbed away. It left Joe feeling about as jolly as yesterday's mashed potatoes. He was lonely, and he wanted his Mum and Dad.

Pulling himself together, Joe decided that he would feel better for a meal. He would make a fire, too – that would cheer him up a bit. As he began to search the shore above the water-line for driftwood, Sheba trotted up, licking his hands as he patted her head. She had guarded Joe well as he slept, and had had a nap herself. Now she felt like play!

Joe found a good stick for her and threw it far along the beach. Sheba tore after it, brought it back and dropped it at Joe's feet. That was the trouble

23

with this game – once Sheba started chasing sticks, she never tired of it.

Joe gathered a big armful of dry wood, whistled for Sheba, and looked around for a good place to make a fireplace. In a sandy hollow, sheltered from the wind by great rocks, Joe built a good big square of stones. Inside this he made a pyramid of thin, dry sticks, then piled a few of the thicker sticks around and above it. He hadn't been in the Cubs for nothing!

Joe felt in his pocket for matches. At the third match, the little pile of twigs caught fire, and Joe proudly watched the flames lick hungrily towards the thicker sticks. What was it about a warm, crackling fire that made you feel more cheerful? Joe asked himself, feeding the flames with more firewood.

Feeling hungry, Joe dug into his rucksack for the tin-opener and had opened a tin of beans before he realised that he had no pan to warm them in! This was a setback but, deciding that he would try anything once, he pushed the tin itself into the edge of the fire.

It was not a very good meal. Joe started badly by burning his fingers on the tin, then found that the beans at the bottom were burnt, and those at the top of the tin were still cold. There was no butter for his bread. Still, it went a long way towards satisfying Joe's hunger, and he finished off with a wedge of his mother's fruit cake, washed down with lemonade.

Sheba gave a short bark as she watched Joe eat a biscuit. Joe laughed at her.

'You're always after my biscuits,' he said.

'Woof,' said Sheba at once, pricking up her ears at the word 'biscuits'. Joe tossed her one, and she crunched it up at once, then looked at him hopefully again.

'No fear,' he told her. 'Biscuits are too precious to waste on you – one gulp and they're gone. You're not supposed to have this kind, anyway – you'll get fat.'

After his meal, Joe set out to explore, with Sheba running joyfully ahead. Before they had gone very far, Joe spotted a little stream which ambled gently around the edge of a field, towards the sea. Sheba began to drink at once, as she was thirsty again. Joe had been rather worried about finding water for her, and he was very relieved. What a smashing place this was – it seemed to have everything!

The nearest road would be about a mile away, Joe thought, and there were no noisy piers or amusement arcades. The little cove was quite deserted, and Joe could almost believe that he and Sheba were alone together on a desert island.

He could just see the roofs of farm buildings up in the hills, about half a mile away, but probably farmers had no time to spare for walking on the beach. In the other direction he could see a wisp of smoke rising lazily in the distance. There must be houses there, but they were a long way off. Joe felt that, for the time being, anyway, Sheba would be quite safe here.

As he walked, Joe worriedly slashed at the grass and shrubs with a stick. Try as he would, he could not stop his mind from wandering back home. His parents would be in such a stew about him. Almost, Joe wished he hadn't run away – but the thing was done now. Flinging himself down on the coarse grass of the sand dunes, he wondered what his mother and father would be doing right now. He wondered whether the police had traced the van driver yet, and talked to the woman at the transport café.

What was going to happen to him? How long would he be able to stay here, hidden, with Sheba? His food would not last for more than a couple of days. After that, he would have to venture out, to try to find food somewhere. Joe found his thoughts going round and round in circles and getting nowhere.

Suddenly remembering the bed he had to make, he got up, thankful to have something to do, and began to look around for softer grass to sleep on. This tough, spiky marram grass would not do at all.

He carried armful after armful of soft grass back to his cave until he had a great pile of it. That would be much more comfortable! Joe unrolled his sleeping-bag, put it on the bed of grass, and stretched himself out experimentally. Sheba whined softly, and pawed at him. Surely her master was not going back to bed again so soon!

'Don't worry, girl,' Joe told her. 'I'm just trying out my new bed. What shall we do now?'

There really was not much to do, and Joe had a very long and rather boring afternoon. He was glad when evening came. Perhaps if he had an early night he might be able to forget his pangs of hunger!

To Sheba's disgust, Joe slid into his sleeping-bag and prepared for sleep. This time, he really meant to sleep, so with a great sigh Sheba resigned herself to it and stretched herself across Joe's feet.

It was still not quite dark when Joe woke up again. What had disturbed him? Sheba was not with him. Perhaps she too had been woken by something, and gone out to investigate. But what could it be? Slowly, Joe realised that there was something different about the sounds around him.

There was the restless noise of the sea, waves splashing against rocks. There was the sighing of the wind, magnified in this hollow cave, and the harsh, yelping cry of a gull. And there was the sound of singing.

Joe was sure he was not mistaken. There it was again – borne faintly on the wind. He crawled to the cave entrance and listened. There was no mistake about it. People were singing, and not too far away, either.

Joe stuffed his feet hastily into his rubber-soled trainer shoes, and cautiously walked along the beach, drawn irresistibly by the sound. As he approached Kelwith Cove, Joe saw a crowd of a dozen or so kids, some younger, some a bit older than he was, sitting around a big bonfire on the beach. Sheba joined him, and the two of them stealthily moved into the sand dunes above the beach, where they could see without being seen.

What was that they were singing? Joe had missed the first words, but these, repeated again and again to a catchy tune, he could not miss.

'The Lord has done great things for us, and we are glad,
We are glad!'

Could it be some kind of Sunday school outing he had stumbled on? Joe cautiously watched, as they sang and clapped. He envied them. They looked as if they really *meant* what they were singing, and they really were glad.

Joe felt he had nothing at all to be glad about. He envied them something else, too. Floating across to him from that happy crowd came the savoury smell of fried sausages! Sheba caught it too, and whined softly as if to say, 'Why don't we go and ask them for some!'

Joe could stand it no longer, and he pulled Sheba away. Turning inland, he decided to take a wide detour to avoid being seen – then stopped and stared.

Beyond the sand dunes, nestling in a sheltered valley, was a whole village of blue tents! Right in the centre of a big grassy area was a very large white tent, which seemed to be the focal point of the whole camp. Beyond that was parked a grey minibus. So this was no Sunday school outing – these kids were actually camping within half a mile of him!

Joe's eye caught a movement among the tents, and kept very still. That big white tent must be the camp kitchen, he thought, for a tall, bearded young man came out, carrying a big tray of those delicious sausages. He carried them down towards the beach. There seemed to be no one else in the camp at all.

Hardly daring to breathe, Joe picked his way between the deserted tents, almost tripping over guy ropes in the growing darkness.

The kitchen tent, lit by a pressure lamp, was empty, and there, on a long table, waiting to be taken to the beach, was another tray of sausages.

Joe seized an empty polythene carrier bag and began to tip the hot sausages into it. He looked around and found a bag of fresh rolls, a packet of butter and some bacon. There was a sack of potatoes leaning against the leg of the table, and a couple of dozen joined everything else, all higgledy-piggledy in Joe's carrier. That should keep him going for a few days!

Cautiously, Joe crept to the doorway and peeped out. The singing had stopped. Those kids were probably stuffing themselves with hot sausages and bread rolls, he thought.

The coast was still clear. Joe had never run so fast. He was through the camp, along the beach and back at the cave before his theft had even been discovered.

To Joe and Sheba that night's supper seemed fit for a king. What if the sausages were slightly grubby from sharing the bag with the potatoes? They were still warm, and delicious. When they could eat no more, the boy and his dog stretched themselves out and slept.

CHAPTER 4

JOE
IN DANGER

The following morning, Joe made up his mind to
steer clear of the camp altogether. He simply
couldn't risk being discovered, especially now that
he was a thief as well as a runaway. He and Sheba
together explored the rocky shore in the other
direction.

This was much more interesting. There were
rockpools hiding all kinds of animal life. Joe found
that if he turned over a big rock, he could find lots of
different sea creatures sheltering underneath, like
the beetles and wood lice that hid beneath stones in
his own garden at home. Some of them Joe had
never seen before, even in books.

He amused himself for a long time, trying to
make two crabs race each other, finding starfish in
the rockpools, and seeing how many different kinds
of seaweed there were on the beach.

Towards mid-day, there was a change in the
weather. Dark clouds began to gather on the
horizon, and the sea breeze turned chilly. The tide
had turned, and the white-topped waves which
lapped the beach looked cold and uninviting.

Joe shivered suddenly, and wished he had his
thick jersey with him. The weather had not been a
problem until now. But he could not help
wondering what he would do if there were a real

storm. How would he get his clothes dry? He glanced uneasily at the sky again, and decided that the best place for him and Sheba was the cave. He would gather lots of driftwood together and pile it inside to keep dry. Then he would still be able to make a fire, even if it rained hard.

Whistling for Sheba, Joe raced across the rocks, trying to avoid the strands of slimy seaweed which lay across them, leaping from one to the other.

Suddenly, as he came down awkwardly on the edge of a huge rock, the force of his landing tipped it sideways. Joe's left foot slipped into the crevice between it and the next rock. He cried out in pain as the great boulder tipped back again, trapping his foot.

As the pain in his ankle slowly subsided, Joe pulled at the foot that was caught. But it was wedged tight.

He sat down on the rock and rested for a minute. Then he tried again. It was no use. The big rock would not budge. He could not free his foot.

Joe untied the lace of his canvas shoe. Perhaps he could slip his foot out of it. He pulled and pushed, twisted and turned, but it was no good.

As Joe looked hopelessly around him, he gradually became aware of a new danger. Right beside him was a good-sized rockpool. A couple of tiny crabs and some shellfish were waiting there for the tide to come up, so that they could escape back to the sea.

The tide!

He turned to look at the threatening waves, coming up fast towards him, now only a matter of feet away. What if he couldn't get his foot free? But he *must* get it free – he was well below the water-line!

Sheba nosed around him in a worried way, wondering why Joe was sitting there in the cold.

Didn't he know that it would be much warmer in the cave?

With mounting panic, Joe tugged at his leg again, with all his strength. The trapped foot didn't even move! Now it was a race against the tide, and all the time the deadly green waves crept nearer and nearer. Joe, panting now with the effort, saw himself being slowly covered by the cold sea. First his legs, then his body ...

'Help!' he cried. 'Help me, someone!'

But Joe had chosen his hiding-place well. Across the hills, a wisp of smoke rising from a house in a hidden valley was the only sign of life. There was no one near enough to help.

Sheba whined, and licked Joe's face and hands. He put his arms around the faithful dog.

'Oh Sheba, what will happen to you if I can't get away?' he said, running his fingers through her silky coat. She looked at him with eyes full of trouble.

The first wave splashed Joe's feet.

'Help!' he cried in desperation.

His voice sounded thin and reedy in the wind. The dismal, mocking cry of a sea bird was his only reply.

'Oh, someone, please come!' he sobbed.

Sheba whined again and licked him all over. Her master was in trouble. What could she do for him? With a parting lick, she bounded away over the rocks.

'Sheba! Sheba – don't leave me!' shouted Joe. 'Come back!' But she was gone.

It was worse without Sheba; Joe had never felt so alone in his life. Where had she gone? He wouldn't have thought she would have deserted him like that ...

Even as he called after her, cold water flooded the rock where Joe sat. In blind panic he pulled desperately at his leg, sobbing, bruising his foot, scraping the skin off his ankle and grazing his knuckles. The rock resisted all his efforts. The sun was gone now, and the sky grew dark as the grey storm clouds piled up.

There was a sudden flash of lightning and, a short time after, thunder rumbled in the distance. The cold wind whipped a spray of salt water into his face, and raised goose bumps on his arms.

And the menacing sea came on, relentlessly.

*　　　*　　　*

Sheba tore along the shore, barking loudly. Joe was in danger. She had to help him somehow. The cove was deserted, but the dog remembered the tents, and the people on the sand around the bonfire. Where there were people, help could be found for Joe. On and on she raced, around the cove, hampered by the deep, soft sand. Through the sand dunes she ran, and into the camp, barking as if her throat would burst.

The first drops of rain were beginning to fall. In the camp three or four boys were rapidly moving their belongings into tents to keep dry. And a young woman and two girls were scurrying about, arms full of half-dry washing snatched from the makeshift clothes-lines, dropping pegs as they went. They all turned in amazement as Sheba burst into camp.

'Where did he spring from?' said one of the boys. 'I haven't seen him around before.' He whistled, and held out his hand to her.

Sheba ran towards him, barking, then back a little way towards the beach. She turned to see if he was following. How stupid these humans seemed to be at times!

'What do you think he wants?' asked a tall girl

33

with freckles. 'Shall I give him something to eat?'

The woman tossed her armful of washing into one of the tents, and called Sheba to her. She crouched down to pat the friendly dog.

'What is it, then?' she said. Sheba tugged feverishly at the leg of her jeans.

'Steve!' she called, suddenly. 'Steve – I think someone needs help.'

Immediately, a tent flap was lifted and her husband's head appeared. It was the bearded man Joe had seen the night before with the tray of sausages.

'What's going on?' he shouted. 'Don't mess about, you lot – get all that gear stowed away. Look at those clouds – it's really going to come down in a minute.'

'Steve!' his wife called again. 'There's a dog here. Come and see – I think he wants us to follow him.'

Steve crawled from his tent. Sheba barked frantically and raced towards the beach, looking back at them hopefully. Steve caught the dog's urgency, and wasted no time.

'Andrew – get a blanket,' he ordered sharply. He called to the two biggest boys. 'Ian and Neil, come with me. Liz, you and the girls get some kettles of water boiling. Let's hope it won't be necessary, but we'll have to make sure.'

All three of them struggled into kagouls, and hurried after Sheba. Through the sand dunes, and along the shore she led them. She was impatient at their slowness, though they were going as fast as they could. And she ran on ahead, barking sharply.

How much further? The rain suddenly came down in sheets, and the rising wind flung it spitefully into their faces. It was like trying to see in a thick fog. The driving rain obliterated everything. Where had the dog gone? Had they lost her?

34

'There she is!' Ian pointed towards the oncoming waves, shouting to make himself heard above the wind. The lightning flashed again, and there was a fearful clap of thunder.

Neil grabbed Steve's arm.

'There's a boy on the rocks down there!' he yelled. 'Right in the water!'

The three picked their way carefully over the wet and slippery rocks. Joe saw them coming, and nearly wept with relief.

'I'm trapped!' he shouted. 'I can't get away!'

Steve moved cautiously down to help Joe, who was now waist deep in water. He rolled up his sleeve and felt below the water to see exactly how and where Joe's foot was held.

'Right,' Steve directed. 'When I give the word, you two heave the rock down to tip it towards you.' He put an arm round Joe's trembling shoulders.

'We'll have you out of there in a jiffy,' he said encouragingly. 'OK,' he shouted. 'Now!'

The two boys pressed down on the rock with all their weight and it tipped easily towards them. Steve eased Joe's foot from the crevice.

They half-carried Joe, his bare arms almost blue with the cold, teeth chattering, drenched by the sea and rain, but faint with relief, to the beach above the water-line. There they wrapped up the shivering boy like a mummy in the blanket. Steve and Neil, with Sheba at their heels, used their arms as a chair-lift for Joe, while Ian ran ahead, to turn the camp kitchen into an emergency hospital.

Sheba trotted after Joe, well satisfied, not minding the steady downpour, though the rain ran from her coat in rivulets. She was content. Joe was safe.

CHAPTER 5

FIRST AID
AND GRASSHOPPERS

An inflatable mattress had been found for Joe, and
put down in a corner of the kitchen tent. He soon
found himself wearing somebody's spare jeans and a
thick jersey. Warm blankets were piled around him
– he'd gone very pale – and a mug of hot, sweet tea
was pushed into his hands. Liz carefully slid the hurt
foot from his shoe.

'Oh, you poor thing!' she cried as she pulled off
Joe's wet sock. His ankle was badly swollen and the
foot already turning blue and green.

The kitchen tent was filling up with sympathetic
onlookers.

'Gosh, that looks awful,' said Neil, bending over
Joe. 'Can you move it about?'

Joe found that he could move it but, when he
did, it was like having red-hot needles pushed into
his ankle. He decided not to try it again!

'However did you come to get your foot stuck
there?' asked Andrew.

'Where do you live?' interrupted another boy.

'What's your name?' said the girl with freckles.

'Joe,' said Joe.

'Karen – leave him alone!' Liz told her, sternly.
'All of you, leave him alone.' She shooed them out
of the tent. 'What Joe needs right now is some peace
and quiet, and a good rest. Then we may have to
take him to a hospital,' she said.

'Oh no,' said Joe firmly.

Liz turned to him.

'Now, don't you start being awkward,' she said. 'This foot doesn't look so good to me – you may have broken a bone.'

'I don't want to go to hospital,' said Joe, getting quite agitated.

If that happened, Sheba would be found and destroyed! He couldn't let that happen! What a fix he was in. Joe buried his head in his hands.

Steve put a kindly hand on his shoulder.

'Look, Joe,' he said. 'Don't worry about it – just rest and get warm, then we'll see. Your ankle may be quite all right after a rest. We probably won't have to worry about hospitals.'

Joe looked up at Steve, who nodded reassuringly. The steady brown eyes made Joe feel that here was someone he could trust. And Joe was very short of friends these days.

'OK,' he said.

A few of the campers still hung about the tent, drawn by the drama.

'And what are you lot waiting for?' Steve said. The youngsters vanished.

Liz, meanwhile, had found the first-aid kit, and was busily unwinding a wide crepe bandage. Joe eyed her nervously.

'What are you going to do?' he said.

She smiled at him, her eyes full of fun.

'Don't worry, I'm not going to hurt you,' she said. 'I'm learning first aid, and I need someone to practise on. I thought you'd do nicely.'

As she bent over his hurt foot, a strand of fair hair fell into her eyes, and she sat up again to push it into the dark blue spotted scarf she had knotted around her head. She gave Joe a quick, impish grin, and winked at him.

Joe found he couldn't help liking these two – Steve and Liz. There was something about them – he couldn't quite put his finger on it.

Liz bandaged his foot up tightly, yet so gently that Joe only winced when she reached the badly grazed ankle-bone. She spread soothing ointment on some gauze, covered the raw ankle, and went on expertly bandaging.

After pinning everything neatly with a safety-pin, she wetted the whole area with water. It was so cold, it took Joe's breath away. Then she made him put his foot up on a pillow so that it would be higher than his head, and tucked him warmly into the blankets.

'We're going to leave you on your own now for a rest,' Steve told him, squatting down beside his mattress. 'But before I go, I'm going to pray for you.'

Joe was very surprised, but he closed his eyes.

'Father, you know all about everyone of us, and you know Joe's troubles. Show him the answer to his problems, and make his ankle completely right again. Amen.'

Joe had never heard anyone pray like that before – as if they knew God like you could know Jim Smith next door. No – closer even than that. How had Steve known he had problems? He hadn't told him anything. But how right Steve was.

Perhaps God could help? Nobody else could, that was for sure! But how could even God sort out the mess he was in? Joe sighed. The worry inside him felt like a lead weight.

Rain still drummed heavily on the canvas roof of the tent, like someone throwing gravel, and thunder grumbled again, a long way off now.

Joe had been quite sure that he would never be able to sleep. But, gradually, a pleasant warmth from the hot tea and cosy blankets stole over him. His eyes closed again.

Sheba, still on sentinel duty beside him, relaxed as Joe drifted into sleep. Her own eyes closed. She had had a busy day.

*   *   *

In his dream, Joe could see himself vividly, walking down a long, straight road with Sheba, on her lead, trotting beside him. Suddenly, Joe looked over his shoulder and fear gripped him. He saw a burly man in a white coat following them, a hypodermic needle in his hand. 'Give the dog to me, boy,' he was saying, coaxingly, 'it won't take a minute. The dog's a killer.'

At the end of the road, strangely enough, Joe could see the blue tents of the camp. Steve was standing in the doorway of the big white kitchen tent. Joe knew somehow that he and Sheba would be safe, if only he could reach the camp. The white-coated man was drawing nearer and nearer, but as Joe turned to run, he realized with horror that his foot was caught between two great paving-stones, and he couldn't move. He rolled over, woke up suddenly and sat up, his heart pounding, breathless and drenched with perspiration.

Neil was shaking his shoulder.

'Are you all right?' he asked, anxiously.

'What?' said Joe, rubbing his eyes.

'You were calling for your dog,' Neil told him. 'She's here – quite safe.'

'Just a bad dream,' said Joe, dismissing it. He wiggled his foot experimentally. 'Hey, my foot's a lot better now.' He pulled back the blankets and tried to stand up.

Liz came in at that moment and caught him.

'What are you doing out of bed?' she said sternly. 'You mustn't put your weight on that foot yet.'

'But it's a lot better now,' protested Joe. 'I can't stay in bed all the time.'

'Give him a camp stool, someone,' said Steve, who had heard him, coming into the kitchen with a pail half full of water. A small, rather wet crowd began to gather, dripping on the black groundsheet. It was still raining, though the heavy downpour had slowed now to a quiet drizzle.

The work-party, boys as well as girls, began to prepare the evening meal. They all seemed to have their own jobs to do. Neil dragged out a sack of potatoes, and Joe blushed at the memory of how he had helped himself from that same sack.

He glanced around the tent. There was the long table which had held trays of sausages. It was now being laid for a meal, and a long bench had been pulled up to it. There was another table in the tent, which held portable gas rings. Three girls were there, frying something which smelled good in an enormous frying-pan.

High up in the tent, an ingenious clothes line had been rigged up, close enough to catch the heat from the cookers, yet not near enough for clothes to catch fire if they should suddenly drop off. From this line hung his own and Steve's wet jeans, and his shirt, stirring gently and steaming as the warm air rose from the gas rings.

Someone pushed a knife into Joe's hand, bringing his mind back to the meal in preparation.

'I never peeled potatoes before,' he protested, looking with distaste at sack and bucket.

'Think what fun you'll have learning,' said Karen unsympathetically. Joe began to chop half-heartedly.

'Look here. There'll be no potato left if you hack great chunks like that off it,' said Peter, one of the older boys. 'Look, do it like this.'

Joe soon got the hang of his new job and, one by one, the potatoes plopped into the bucket, white and shiny, like mis-shapen golf balls.

'That's a smashing dog you've got,' said Andrew, digging an eye out of the potato he was peeling. 'Do you realise that you wouldn't be here now if she hadn't run to fetch us.' He reached out to fondle Sheba's long and silky ears. She had soon become a firm favourite with them all.

'God must have had a special reason for saving your life,' put in Neil. That was a queer way for a boy to talk, Joe thought.

'I wish I had a dog like that,' said Peter.

'She's ace,' said Joe, wishing with all his heart that Sheba was quite safe.

A pretty girl with dark curly hair, came into the tent with kettles of water, and set them to boil on a two-burner gas ring. Peter immediately sat up to watch her, a mischievous gleam in his eye. The others, knowing the signs, began to nudge one another.

'What's the matter?' said Joe.

'Sh!' said Karen.

'You watch Wendy make the tea,' whispered Neil, who was sitting next to him. 'Judging by the look on Peter's face, he's about to play a trick on her. You'll have to keep an eye on that guy – he's always playing some practical joke or other. He put worms in my shoes last night.'

Karen chuckled. 'Do you remember the time he glued some money to the club floor?' she said. 'We counted fifteen people who tried to pick it up and couldn't!'

'Look out,' said Peter softly, his face full of

suppressed laughter, as Wendy lifted the great brown enamel teapot on to the table. As she lifted the lid, a large and lively grasshopper jumped suddenly into her face. She screamed, and dropped the teapot with a loud crash as more and more grasshoppers followed, springing out of the pot as though fired from a catapult. It was like watching a jack-in-a-box gone mad. Peter's shout of laughter was infectious, and soon Joe, like the rest, was holding his sides, tears of laughter streaming down his face.

'Look at them go!' chuckled Neil weakly, wiping his eyes. The black ground-sheet was alive with the hopping, jumping insects. Steve was on his knees, grabbing at them as they passed him. Karen was standing, horror stricken, on the only chair in the tent.

'Get rid of them!' she squealed. 'Get them out, quick! Ooh! One's gone in with the potatoes!'

Wendy, after her first startled scream, had disappeared altogether. As the last grasshopper was captured, order was restored, and Wendy, much shaken, was found and brought back to the kitchen.

'Pest!' she said to Peter. 'I hate grasshoppers!'

'I'm sorry, Wendy – really I am,' Peter told her, but with a suspicious shake in his voice. 'I didn't know they'd scare you as much as that!'

In spite of Peter's apologies, both he and the other boys had a tendency, as they worked, to choke every now and then, and giggle whenever they caught each other's eye.

CHAPTER 6

AWKWARD QUESTIONS

The rain had stopped completely now, and a watery sun struggled to break through the cloud. In spite of the grasshoppers, the meal was a good one: beefburgers, beans and potatoes, eaten in the fresh air on a huge tarpaulin which had been spread on the wet grass, with nobody bothering too much about table manners.

Joe, faced with his first square meal since leaving home, was ravenous. But during the meal came the questions he had been dreading.

'Where are you from, Joe?' asked Andrew.

'Oh, not far away,' Joe stalled. 'Just a few miles from here. I'm staying in a cave near here, birdwatching,' he said untruthfully.

'Oh, I'm keen on birds myself,' broke in James, one of the younger boys. You would be, thought Joe, who knew next to nothing about birds. He wished he had chosen to be beachcombing instead.

'Seen anything interesting?' James went on. 'Last holidays we went to Anglesey, and there were tons of puffins near a lighthouse there. And razorbills and cormorants too.'

'Oh, lots of different gulls, of course, and a puffin or two,' answered Joe airily, inventing as he went.

'Puffins! Here?' cried James eagerly. 'Wow! I'll

come with you to see them one day. You will take me, won't you? Are they far away from the camp?'

Joe was saved by Steve, who came over and sat down with the two boys. He asked Joe what kind of games he liked. Here Joe was in his element, and chattered away happily about his chances of swimming for the school, and the possibility of making the football team next season.

As the evening went on, the last of the clouds blew away and the sun, now setting, shone again on the camp. Steve and Peter brought out guitars, and they all gathered round in a circle for campfire songs.

Joe didn't know the words of the songs they sang. But when someone struck up, 'The Lord has done great things for us,' Joe remembered it from the night before, and joined in.

There was something different about these kids, Joe told himself as he sang, la–la-ing where he didn't know the words. They seemed to have got religion – but it was a kind he had never met up with before. There were no long faces here – in fact, these kids seemed to have more fun and enjoy life more than other people.

Joe couldn't make it out at all. Take Steve and Liz, for example. Joe had never met a nicer pair. Why, they acted as though they really cared about him – yet he had only known them for a few hours. Joe suddenly remembered the food he had stolen from them, and wriggled uncomfortably. They must never get to know that he, Joe, was the thief. How much would they care about him then?

So many things to hide! So many lies to remember! Black thoughts whirled and tumbled in Joe's brain, making him dizzy. Suddenly, he felt dog-tired. His foot throbbed painfully and his head ached.

That night, he shared Andrew's tent. To his surprise, he slept better than he had done for a long time. The others slept well, too, tired out by the long day and the fresh air.

Steve and Liz sat together by the dying campfire, enjoying a last mug of cocoa.

'I like that young Joe, don't you?' said Liz suddenly. 'What did you make of his story?' She idly twirled a strand of her hair round and round her finger.

'Not a lot,' he replied. 'About one word in every ten might be true! Puffins indeed!' he snorted. 'I'd as soon believe there were penguins hopping up and down the rocks! That boy's in some kind of trouble – I can see it in his eyes. There's fear in his face. That's not normal for a twelve-year-old boy.' He drained his mug and set it down on the grass. 'We'll have to help him all we can.'

'I wonder if he'll let us?' said Liz, softly.

*   *   *

Life in camp with these kids was much more fun than living alone in the cave. Joe found himself watching Peter, who kept the campers on their toes with a constant succession of jokes and tricks.

Steve and Liz found him most tiresome. And the girls kept a very wary eye on him – they were usually on the receiving end of his sense of humour. But the boys loved every one of his tricks and watched eagerly for the next one.

Only the night before, Karen had found a crab (very dead), in her sleeping-bag. Andrew claimed that his stomach had been damaged for life after drinking a cup of tea made with salt instead of sugar. Steve was presented with a pencil whose point was made of rubber and wobbled about mysteriously!

Even Joe was not left out.

Boiled eggs appeared for breakfast that morning, and everyone was soon hungrily tucking in. Joe chopped at the top of his egg only to find that Peter, who was doing the serving that day, had given him an uncooked one. Yellow yolk cascaded down the sides of the egg cup and trickled stickily along the boards of the big table, making a dreadful mess. Peter shook with laughter. Liz was quite cross.

'What a crazy thing to do, Peter,' she said. 'Won't you ever grow up? Go and get a cloth, and clean up that mess. Then you can get poor Joe some more breakfast – *without* worms, crabs or grass-hoppers, please!'

Still chuckling, Peter went off to do as he was told, and, though he smelled everything suspi-ciously, Joe could find nothing else wrong with the breakfast he was given at last.

After breakfast came morning prayers. Most of the camp joined in – even young James who was only nine – all talking to God in the same confident way that Steve had done the day before. Joe had been included in a very friendly way in everything they did. Yet here was something he couldn't share – some secret which they were a part of, and he wasn't.

The chores came next, and everyone had his own job to do, clearing dishes, washing up, washing out tea-towels and socks.

Joe was told to sit down for a while, and though he argued that his foot was almost quite all right again, Liz told him sternly that it still needed rest. He climbed one of the nearby sand-dunes, barely limping at all now, and relaxed in the gentle warmth of the sun, watching the bustle in the camp below him.

Before long, Steve wandered up and flopped down beside Joe. He put his arms behind his head

48

and leaned back comfortably, stretching out his long legs.

'It's nice to be able to relax for a few minutes,' he said to Joe. 'Camping's jolly hard work.'

Joe nodded. 'Do you camp here a lot?' he asked.

'Every year, in the Spring holidays,' said Steve.

'Our school doesn't break up till next week,' Joe observed, and immediately could have bitten off his tongue, knowing at once what Steve's next question would be. It came.

'So you're supposed to be at school? Is this an extra holiday, then, or what?'

Joe murmured something about having been ill, and needing a break. But he found he couldn't meet Steve's eye. He changed the subject.

'Everybody seems to be having a smashing time here,' he said.

'Oh, we always do,' said Steve enthusiastically. 'We have some good times together at home too, you know. We're all from a church near London – we call ourselves the Pioneers.'

'Oh,' said Joe.

'Where are you from, Joe?' asked Steve.

Joe hesitated before he replied. He must be very careful what he said – it wouldn't be easy to pull the wool over Steve's eyes!

'Oh, a village not far away,' he said, at last. 'I don't suppose you'd know it.'

'I don't suppose I would,' said Steve, looking directly at Joe – and the friendly brown eyes somehow made Joe feel uncomfortable. It almost seemed as if Steve knew, without being told, that he had something to hide. He had a sudden urge to tell Steve everything – he desperately needed help from somewhere. But even Steve would be sure to tell him to go back home – he might even hand him over to the police!

Unexpectedly Steve said, 'Do your parents know where you are?'

'Oh, yes,' Joe answered quickly. Rather too quickly, Steve thought. 'I told you, I'm here for a holiday, birdwatching.'

Steve chewed thoughtfully on a piece of grass. 'Yes,' he said. 'I know you told us that. Puffins at Kelwith Cove?'

'Perhaps I made a mistake,' Joe defended himself. 'I daresay they were some other kind of bird.'

Steve chuckled. 'Sure they weren't great auks? Or vultures perhaps?'

Joe wasn't enjoying this conversation. He was annoyed with himself. Why on earth had he chosen to be a birdwatcher, when he knew nothing about birds? Steve touched his arm gently and Joe turned to look at him.

'I wish you'd let me in on your problems, Joe,' he said softly. 'Maybe I could help.'

Joe looked away quickly. 'I don't know what you mean,' he said.

Steve sighed. This was more difficult than he had thought it would be. He decided on a little plain speaking.

'Look, Joe,' he said. 'I know you're not telling me the truth.'

Joe opened his mouth to interrupt, but Steve said, 'Hang on, Joe – let me finish.' Joe looked miserably at the ground. What kind of trouble was he in now? Where would all this end?

'I found your cave this morning,' Steve went on. 'I wanted to bring up your sleeping-bag and anything else you might need. And I found out one or two things about you. The first thing I noticed was that there were no binoculars with your things. No birdwatcher goes out without binoculars! The second thing was that mothers always load up their children with plenty of good grub when they go away for a camping holiday. They don't leave them to take sausages and potatoes that don't belong to them.'

'Oh, no,' groaned Joe, ashamed of himself.

Steve put a kindly arm around the boy's shoulders. 'Those two facts tell me that you are not birdwatching, and that your parents don't know you're here. I'm right, aren't I?'

Joe nodded, too full up to speak.

'You're in some kind of mess, Joe, aren't you?'

Joe nodded again. 'I'm sorry I stole your things,' he said, a catch in his voice. 'You've been good to me.'

'Are you really sorry you stole them?' Steve said quietly. 'Or just sorry you got found out?'

Joe stared. 'I never thought of it like that before,' he said.

Steve gave his shoulder a squeeze. 'Look here, Joe,' he said, 'you don't have to steal from me. If I have anything you need, I'll gladly share it with you. Won't you trust me, and tell me what the trouble is?'

Again, Joe was tempted to tell Steve the whole truth. He hesitated, then looked at Sheba. He was her only protection. His arms went around her, holding her tight, and his head went down until he could feel her silky coat against his cheek. She turned to lick his nose.

'I *can't* tell you,' he said, after a long time. 'I wish I could.' And he found he really meant it.

CHAPTER 7

THE WATCHER
ON THE CLIFF

The campers were packing up the minibus and getting ready for a day out at the zoo. Joe watched, enviously. Liz, who had been counting the bags of sandwiches, came over to him. She had seen the longing in his eyes.

'I wish you could come with us, Joe,' she said. 'But this trip's been booked for a long time, and the minibus is full to bursting already. I don't think we could fit in another sardine! I'm sorry you can't come, though – it's a real shame!'

Joe was sorry, too, but it couldn't be helped. Everyone had been so good at making him feel welcome, and he had been included in everything they had done up to now. He knew that if it had been possible, Steve and Liz would have squeezed him in somewhere.

'Never mind,' said Joe. 'I'll go back to the cave with Sheba for the day. We'll be all right – don't worry about us.'

Liz gave him a cheeky grin. 'Sorry I haven't any sausages and rolls you can have,' she said, teasingly. 'You might find these useful instead.' And she pushed a packet of sandwiches and a huge apple into his hand.

Joe looked sheepish. 'Don't remind me of that,' he told her. 'I wouldn't have pinched them if I'd known you.'

Steve, already in the driving-seat and anxious to be off, gave his wife a short toot on the horn.

'I must go,' she said. 'Have a good day, and don't do too much walking on that foot!'

'Come on, Liz!' shouted Steve. She clambered with difficulty into the crowded bus, and the door slammed shut behind her.

'Have a good time!' shouted Joe, as Steve put the engine into gear and drew away, rather bumpily over the uneven ground. The windows were a forest of waving hands.

Joe, left alone, wondered how he was going to occupy himself for a whole day. He had come to rely so much on his new friends. How would he get on when their holiday came to an end, and they had to leave for good?

Then, a new thought struck him. As soon as the campers reached home, they would be sure to hear about the search for a missing boy and his dog. They printed things like that in the newspapers, didn't they? All the kids knew his name, and Sheba's. They knew where the cave was.

With a sinking heart, Joe realised that as soon as they left, he and Sheba would have to leave, too. Where else could he find as good a hiding-place? He just *had* to keep Sheba out of the way of the police! What a good thing that none of the children seemed to have a radio with them, or they might already have found out who he was, from news-flashes or something.

Sheba gave a sudden bark – the kind of bark she used when she was excited or disturbed.

'What is it, girl?' said Joe, patting her big head. She barked again, and then Joe heard it, too. Her sharp ears had caught the regular throbbing beat of a helicopter, flying low down and coming this way. Joe squinted up into the sky, shielding his eyes from the glare of the sun.

There it was, carefully following a course along the ins and outs of the shore-line. It was as if the pilot were looking for something. Joe wondered, for a minute, what could be the matter – then he knew, suddenly, that he was the one they were hunting!

The helicopter was very close now, and coming fast. Could he get to cover in time? He thought he could just do it.

Joe raced towards the nearest tent, with Sheba, barking madly, at his heels, and flung himself inside, twisting his ankle again as he came down with a crash, but hardly noticing the pain. He grabbed the collar of the surprised dog and hauled her in after him.

Would the pilot have spotted them – or had they made it in time? The helicopter seemed to hang about deliberately, and it seemed like a lifetime to poor Joe before the deafening thump of the engine faded into the distance. Perhaps it seemed longer, not being able to see what was happening.

Badly scared, Joe stayed in the tent for a long time before he dared to crawl out again. What if the helicopter came back and caught him in the open, where he could be seen?

But he couldn't stay in the tent all day, and Sheba was already wondering how much longer they would have to crouch in this funny little place, when they could be out of doors in the sunshine. After thinking it out, Joe decided that the safest thing for him to do would be to keep to the shore. The helicopter had already searched there once. It would surely turn inland after finding nothing by the seaside!

He picked his way through the sand dunes, with their coarse, wiry grass, which lay between the camp and the sea-shore, and set out for the cave. He had not been there since his accident, and the distance, about a quarter of a mile, was not enough to make his foot any worse.

As he walked, he whistled the catchy tune of 'The Lord has done great things for us' – then stopped abruptly. His heart began to beat uncomfortably fast. Fresh footprints led straight towards the mouth of the cave. He fitted his own foot to one of them, though he knew before he did so, it would be far too small.

His own prints were there too – plenty of them, but his small foot had never made these! A man had been here! Then he relaxed again, as he remembered that Steve had been down to collect his sleeping-bag and things.

As he bent to enter the low cave the first thing Joe noticed, lying right by the entrance, was a cigarette end. Steve did not smoke. Prickles ran up and down his spine, and his mouth went suddenly dry, as he realised that a stranger had been here.

Joe hunted among his things which were still piled against the back wall of the cave, in case anything had been stolen. Steve had taken his clothes and Sheba's tins of meat away, but the rest of his belongings –and even the stolen potatoes and bread rolls, hard and stale now – all seemed to be there.

No – his map was missing. He tipped everything out of the rucksack and had a proper look, but there was no map there. Joe sat back on his heels, wondering. Why would anyone want to steal a map? It was a very old one of his father's, well worn and rather dog-eared. Perhaps Steve had picked it up with his clothes by mistake?

Joe sat down on the heap of grass, now dead and dry, which had been his bed. He simply must think this out. Sheba pawed at his legs, impatiently. She didn't like all this sitting around! Joe fondled her ears affectionately.

'All right then, girl – come on ! It's a walk you want, isn't it? Let's follow that line of footprints, and see where they go!'

Sheba bounded on ahead, glad to be going somewhere. The tide was in, and the big dog splashed joyfully in and out of the gentle waves, chasing pebbles which Joe threw for her.

Joe followed the footprints easily for a while. On and on they went, showing clearly in the soft sand above the water-line. When Joe reached the shingly part of the beach, the prints were much harder to follow – just one every now and again on an odd sandy bit. Then he came to a standstill.

Rocks now stretched ahead of him, on to the point, where the land jutted into the sea, and the cliff rose steeply from the wild and rocky shore. Joe wondered why the man had not turned off the beach before this. The going was very rough across the slippery, seaweedy rocks. No more footprints could be found, of course. Joe turned back again, disappointed, his detective work at an end.

*　　　*　　　*

A watcher on the cliff, far above him, trained a pair of powerful binoculars on Joe. They held steady for half a minute, then swept the beach until they found Sheba, trotting ahead of her young master.

The man lowered the binoculars, a satisfied smile on his face, and turned away.

*　　　*　　　*

Steve and Liz, with the campers, had a wonderful day at the zoo. They had pony rides. They watched the fierce lions being fed, and bought peanuts for the monkeys. They enjoyed seeing the snakes in the reptile house. Some of them were very poisonous. They certainly didn't envy the keeper who had to feed them, and clean out the cages! A friendly keeper was handling a small python, and he let them stroke its smooth, shiny skin.

Karen said, 'I always thought snakes were nasty slimy things.'

'Oh, no,' the keeper said, quite shocked. 'It's amazing how many people think that. There are some very beautiful snakes and pythons – I love them all.' He was obviously very fond of his python, and even allowed Peter to take hold of it and let it wind itself about his arm.

'Do be careful, Peter,' said Wendy. 'They can squeeze you to death!'

The keeper chuckled. 'Not this one – he's about big enough to kill a rat or a squirrel, but not a big hunk of beef like this chap!' They all laughed.

After their picnic lunch came the afternoon dolphin show. And what a marvellous show it was! They had never seen anything like these graceful dolphins before. Up they leapt from the water, through a hoop, then dropped smoothly back again. In and out they went, leaping and diving, skilfully taking fish from the hand of their trainer in the middle of a jump. Everyone was sad when it was all over – they could have stayed for the rest of the day watching these clever animals.

Steve glanced at his watch as they all filed out of the entrance to the dolphin pool.

'Just about time for a drink,' he said. 'Then we must be off. It's quite a long drive back to camp.'

'Here's a shop,' shouted James. 'I'm going to buy some rock for Joe with the name of the zoo all the way through the middle.'

Next door to the gift shop was a self-service café, with noisy music spilling from a radio. They were glad of the chance to sit down again and rest their weary feet. They trooped inside. Steve ordered tea for himself and Liz, and colas all round for the rest.

'Ooby-dooby shal-a-la,' a woman's voice burbled to a background of electric guitars. 'I love you, I love you, I love you, I do.'

'Really,' muttered Andrew.

'Well, we've had a smashing day out, haven't we?' said Steve.

'What time will we get back to the camp?' asked James, who badly wanted to give his stick of rock to Joe.

Steve looked at his watch again. 'We came the long way round, so I reckon we should be home by ...'

Liz suddenly grabbed his arm. 'Sh!' she said.

'What's wrong, love? There's no need to ...'

'Hush a minute, Steve.'

A newsreader had replaced the raucous singer, and was in the middle of a sentence.

' ... now the fourth day since this boy was last seen in a transport café near the village of Byford Green. He is thought to be in hiding somewhere with his dog, a red setter. Police and searchers are anxious to find Joe and the dog, as the animal is described as being a savage sheep-killer. Another car crash today at a notorious accident blackspot ...'

'Oh, poor Joe!' cried Liz. 'And that lovely dog!'

'A savage sheep-killer? Sheba?' said Andrew fiercely. 'She *can't* be!'

'Hang on, Andrew,' cautioned Steve. 'It's perfectly possible. An awful lot of nice dogs do turn to chasing sheep if they're not trained properly. I don't know whether Sheba is really a killer dog or not. One thing I do know, though; Joe's in real trouble.'

58

'What do you think we can do to help him?' said Liz. She had taken a real liking to the lonely boy.

Steve pushed back his chair abruptly, making it squawk loudly on the tiled floor. 'I don't know yet,' he said. 'Let's get going.'

CHAPTER 8

WHERE IS SHEBA?

Joe was very bored. Idly, he built a pyramid of small pebbles, then savagely kicked it down again, scowling. There wasn't much to do on your own at the seaside. The idea of going for a swim crossed his mind. But, in spite of the sunshine, a sneaky wind made the waves look cold and uninviting.

He tried playing a word game, saying the name of a town, then trying to think of another one beginning with the last letter of the town. 'London …Newcastle, Edinburgh,' he muttered, 'Hull, Leicester, Reading.' But he stuck fast at G. The game was no fun alone, anyway.

Joe sat down on the warm sand, leaning against the sandy bank behind him, and closed his eyes against the glare of the sun. He had not meant to fall asleep, but when he opened his eyes again he felt chilled, and the sun had clouded over.

He was quite alone – Sheba must have gone off on some excursion of her own. He wondered what the time was, and wished he hadn't left his watch in Andrew's tent. Anyway, it must be way past lunch-time, and he hadn't eaten his sandwiches yet.

Joe was half-way through his meal when it occurred to him that Sheba was a long time away. She often left him to go exploring by herself, but she was never away for long. He called to her.

'Sheba! Sheba – here, girl!' But there was no wel-
come, answering bark. Joe felt suddenly alarmed.
His food forgotten, he began to search the beach.
Sheba's pawmarks were everywhere in the soft sand.
So were his own footprints. But there seemed to be
no clue as to which way she had gone.

Then Joe's heart almost stood still as he spotted,
further down the beach and half-covered in sand, a
small piece of raw meat. He did some fast thinking.

Someone, probably realizing that Sheba was the
dog wanted by the police, had seen her on the beach,
and enticed her away from Joe as he slept. Why on
earth had he let himself drop off like that? Joe
blamed himself bitterly. That someone must have
lured her away with the meat, captured her as she
was eating, and taken her away. But where to?

The man, if it was a man, must have come, and
gone, through the sand dunes, as there were few new
footprints in the sand. And the grassy dunes, of
course, showed no marks at all. Joe looked around
him in desperation. There was nothing at all to help
him. No clue except the prints which he had already
followed once that morning, without success.

Wherever the man had taken Sheba, it was not
that way. The same line of deep footprints still led
away along the beach towards the dangerous, rocky
point. But Joe had a feeling about those footprints.
Somehow, he had a hunch that he was on the right
track. He would follow them again, but this time he
would carry on across the rocks and round the
headland into the next bay. Perhaps there would be
other clues there to follow? Determinedly Joe set
out.

It was very rough going indeed across the rocks.
The ordeal he had gone through had made Joe very
nervous of this rocky part of the shore. He
shuddered at the nightmare memory of having his

foot trapped between the rocks – and the restless, menacing tide coming nearer all the time. He forced himself to think instead of how Sheba had brought help to him. She had actually saved his life! Joe knew that if she hadn't gone for Steve and the others when she had, he would certainly not be alive at this moment.

Joe rounded the rocky point with difficulty, slowly and carefully picking his way over and between the slimy, seaweed-covered rocks. He was very thankful to see, beyond the rocks, another shingle beach. Once he got there, it would be much easier to get along. As he went, Joe whistled and shouted for Sheba, but there was no sign that anyone had ever crossed these desolate rocks before. He asked himself suddenly if he was on a wild goose chase? But he pressed on anyway.

The cliffs here were sheer, rising steeply from the beach, wild and forbidding. When Joe reached the shingly beach, he was surprised and excited to find a steep staircase cut right into the rock of the cliff-face itself. It was very old indeed; overgrown, slimy green, and slippery in places. Joe thought it had probably been made by fishermen of long ago, or perhaps by the people who farmed the land up in the hills, to give them easy access to the beach.   Joe was drawn to the stairway, as if it were a magnet. Here, perhaps, lay the secret of Sheba's disappearance! Eagerly he started forward and began to climb the steps. They were in a dangerous condition, and more than once he almost lost his footing. He was very relieved when the staircase brought him out onto a narrow footpath which led along the top of the cliff.

What a view there was from up here! Joe could see for miles. The wild wind caught his mop of dark hair, and made his baggy jersey flap about. How strong it was! Much stronger here than down on the beach. The path followed the edge of the cliff for some way, then turned inland and downhill. Joe hoped he was going in the right direction.

Suddenly, he pounced on something which lay at the side of the path, and triumphantly picked up a cigarette end. It was the same brand as the one he had found earlier by the cave entrance! Now he was getting somewhere.

The path was widening now as it approached run-down farm buildings and, instinctively, Joe walked more quietly. The whole place looked somehow forgotten. The big wooden gate, standing open, hung crookedly from one hinge, and had scored a deep curving groove into the mud of the farmyard. Joe felt strangely uneasy as he stood in the lane, in two minds whether he should go in, or not.

There seemed to be nobody about at all. There was no sign of life, not even the usual sheepdog. Yet Joe's heart began to thump uncomfortably as he looked around him. He had the creepy feeling that someone was watching him. But though he carefully scanned the windows of the shabby farmhouse which stared at him vacantly, his keen eyes caught no movement anywhere.

'You're just imagining things, Joe Brooke,' he told himself sternly.

He crouched down to examine the mud of the farmyard. There were the great tyre tracks of a tractor, and many deep footprints – and the pawmarks of a large dog! Joe forgot his fears and shouted.

'Sheba! Sheba!'

A loud and urgent barking answered him, coming from a nearby outhouse. Joe raced over to it, forgetful now of any danger to himself. Sheba was wild with delight, scraping madly at the door and barking joyfully. Joe yanked impatiently at the door, then saw that a padlock hung over the catch, unlocked, yet stopping the door from opening. Joe bent to unfasten it.

A heavy hand on his shoulder suddenly spun him around. Joe caught his breath sharply in dismay. He found himself face to face with a small, thin man, who held him triumphantly in a vice-like grip. Joe would never have guessed, judging by the man's size, that he could have had such strength!

'Ow! Let go my shoulder – you're hurting me!' he cried.

The thin man smiled unpleasantly. 'Now, that's a real shame!' he said, sounding as though he meant just the opposite.

Sheba, hearing her enemy's voice, began to growl savagely, and she flung herself against the outhouse door in rage. What wouldn't she give for a chance to sink her teeth into some soft portion of the man who had dared to lock her up in this place!

The man ignored the angry dog.

'You're trespassing on my land,' he told Joe unpleasantly. 'I'll give you ten seconds to get out of here.'

'I'm not going without my dog,' said Joe promptly, twisting his shoulder away from the man's painful grip. 'You've no right to steal my dog and shut her up in your shed. It's against the law!'

The man turned his watery blue eyes on Joe.

'Go to the police, then, and tell them all about it.' He was enjoying tormenting Joe. 'Ah – you wouldn't do that, would you?' he said.

'I don't know what you mean,' Joe bluffed. The farmer thrust his face close to Joe's.

'Don't give me that!' he said. 'I've got your map with your father's name and address on it. I know exactly who you are!'

So that was why the map had been taken! Joe

stared at the ground miserably.

'That dog's a vicious killer,' the man said, his voice rising. 'Listen to that!' he shouted. Sheba still barked and growled and tore at the door. The pale eyes flickered.

'That's a dangerous animal, and it deserves everything it gets!' His voice sank suddenly to a whisper. 'I cleaned my shotgun especially for this moment!'

'No!' cried Joe in anguish. The farmer must be quite mad!

The man turned to open the outhouse door, and Joe waited expectantly for the angry dog to spring out on her enemy. Grudgingly he marvelled at the small man's courage in facing the big dog so fearlessly. But as Sheba bounded from the shed like a bullet from a gun, the man had overpowered her in a trice and was strapping a muzzle to the snarling jaws. How strong this dreadful man must be!

Before he knew what was happening, Joe found himself being propelled violently through the door and into the dark and foul-smelling shed. The door slammed and he heard the click of the padlock. Joe beat loudly on the door with his fists.

'Let me out!' he shouted. 'Don't you dare hurt my dog! Where are you taking her?'

'Wouldn't you like to know!' said the man, nastily.

'Don't hurt her!' shouted Joe.

'She deserves it,' the man replied, savagely. 'An animal like this who kills sheep for fun should be shot. I think I'll shoot her straight away.' He enjoyed frightening Joe. 'Or on second thoughts, perhaps I'll wait until tomorrow. A night in there won't do you any harm!'

By the outhouse door was a very high window, tiny and extremely dirty. Joe stood on a box and was just in time to see the farmer drag Sheba, still snarling, away towards the farmhouse. He hammered on the wooden wall of the shed, but the man didn't even turn around.

Joe turned to look around him, but could see very little. The window, with its layers of grime, turned the sunny evening into deep twilight. He took off his shoe, turned his face away and bashed at the little window, careless of the consequences, until all the glass had gone. That was much better. he could see what he was doing now.

Joe looked frantically around the shed, in hopes of finding some way out, but there was none. The door remained immovable. The window was far too small. Perhaps there was some tool here that he could use?

Joe hunted about him. The outhouse was mainly a store for large cans of pesticide. Empty sacks hung from rusting nails, and an ancient saddle, green with mildew, hung by the window. The bad smell came from two large sacks of fertilizer in a corner. On a wide shelf there were cans of old paint, several hard and stiff brushes, boxes of nails and screws – and a badly rusted screw-driver.

He seized this at once, and with trembling fingers began to tackle the screws in the hinges of the door. But the tool was too badly rusted, and the edge broke away at the first pressure Joe put on it. He flung it down, impatiently. There had to be some way out! Surely he hadn't protected his dog all this time, only to have her shot by a mad farmer!

The thought of spending the night as a prisoner in this dirty shed, and leaving Sheba at the mercy of that strange man who seemed half-mad, made Joe frantic. He beat wildly again on the door of the shed, shouting at the top of his voice. But he might have been on a desert island for all the response he got.

In despair, he sank down on the box, his head in his hands. How could he spend the night here? But there was no help for it. An eternity passed, it seemed, before the light faded from the sky. The night stretched before him like a prison sentence.

That was the longest, coldest night Joe had ever spent. He slept lightly, woke in the pitch dark, stiff and cramped, slept and woke again. The first light of a chilly dawn found Joe on the earth floor of the outhouse, his arms pillowing his head on the hard box.

He stirred and sat up suddenly, rubbing his aching arms. He wondered dully whether Sheba were dead already, or whether the farmer had decided to leave the shooting until this morning. Joe had no doubt at all in his mind that the farmer would carry out his threat – he had been in deadly earnest.

As if in answer to his unspoken thought, Joe heard a far-away barking from the direction of the farmhouse; rather muffled, it was true, but Joe knew at once it was Sheba's familiar bark. So she was still alive! Perhaps there was yet time to save her! If only he had told Steve all about it when he had the chance, all this would probably have never happened. What would Steve tell him to do right now? he asked himself. Probably tell him to pray, he thought bitterly. But perhaps even that was worth trying. Joe had reached such a point of desperation that he would try anything!

'Oh, God,' he prayed, trying to sound more confident than he felt, 'if you're listening, please show me the way to get out of here. Amen.'

Joe sighed. He did not really believe that God would answer his prayer. Why should he? He had never done anything for God! He wondered how long he would be locked up before the farmer came

to let him out. Sheba would be dead by then, though – he knew he would never be set free while his dog was still alive!

Spurred into fresh action by the thought, but without much hope, he searched the outhouse yet again. He moved boxes and containers, swept aside the tins of paint, looked behind the mouldy saddle. He tore down the old sacks from the wall – and saw an ancient, forgotten axe hanging from the nail beneath them. True, it was very old and rusty – but beneath the rust it was a solid tool.

An uncomfortable lump came into Joe's throat, and his eyes grew suddenly misty. He brushed them impatiently with the back of his hand. There must be something in this prayer business after all!

Feeling decidedly more cheerful, Joe cleared part of the back wall of the shed – the side furthest away from the farmhouse. He didn't want the farmer to see a hole suddenly appearing in his outhouse wall!

Determinedly, Joe took the axe and attacked the old wood, splintering it at the first stroke. Desperately, with all his strength, he struck again and again. Somehow – anyhow – he must get to Steve. Steve would know what to do. Steve would help him to save Sheba!

CHAPTER 9

STEVE AND LIZ STICK THEIR NECKS OUT

Steve pushed the speed of the minibus as hard as he dared on the return journey, his face unusually grim, his hands gripping the wheel tightly. In all his experience, he had never before come across a problem like this one. What in the world could he do to help Joe? If Sheba really was guilty of attacking sheep, it was highly likely she would have to be put down. But it would break young Joe's heart! There must be *something* he could do to help. If ever he prayed for wisdom, Steve prayed now!

The one clear notion that offered itself was that he should let Joe's parents know where he was, and the sooner the better. What unbearable anxiety, not to know whether Joe was alive or dead! Steve knew that he had to put their minds at rest. That much was as plain as a pikestaff. Once his mind was made up, Steve felt he could breathe more freely. Yes. That was the only right thing to do. He turned to his wife.

'Liz – do you remember? Did they give Joe's address over the radio?' he asked her. 'You heard more than I did.'

'Acacia Avenue, Heystock,' Liz said, promptly. 'I remembered it because of Aunt Lorna – she lives in Heystock, you know. But I can't remember the number of Joe's house.'

'Well, this is how I see it,' he told her. 'Joe's parents have a right to know where he is, and we've got to tell them. The only thing is, *I* can't go because I'll be needed in camp. Do you think you could drive out to Heystock first thing in the morning, and bring them down here? You can easily find out the number of the house once you get there. Joe's father is the one who should decide what to do for the best.'

She looked across at him approvingly. 'I always said I married a genius. That's just what's needed. I don't know if Joe would agree, though, he's so terribly worried about Sheba. What do you think will happen to her?'

Steve gently applied the brakes and slowed down as he approached a set of traffic lights which were just about to change to red. He hesitated for a long time. The lights were green again before he replied.

'I'm very much afraid she'll have to be destroyed,' he said at last. 'Sheba's a great dog, but if they've real proof that she is a sheep killer, nothing we could say or do can alter that fact. There's no other way. It's such a pity, after all Joe's done to try to save her, but I honestly believe she'll be put down in the end.'

'There must be some way round it,' Liz argued.

Steve sighed. 'I only wish you were right, love – but look at it logically!'

Liz's old grin appeared for a moment. 'I might just manage that!' she said. 'But where's your faith? Logic or no logic, I believe God has an answer to this problem. If Jesus could turn water into wine 2,000 years ago, to please people at a wedding, then surely he can sort this mess out for Joe, and save Sheba too. God is the same today as he's always been.'

Steve turned to her and grinned affectionately.

71

'OK, you win,' he said. 'I'm with you all the way. So we'll both stick our necks out and believe God together. Right?'

Liz sat back, satisfied. 'Right,' she said. 'And I'm going to tell that to Joe the minute we get back.'

*   *   *

Liz had been so sure that Joe would be there, waiting for the minibus, telling them how quiet it had been all day; asking what they had done at the zoo. She gazed around the empty camp with a troubled face. Where could he be?

But meals have to be cooked even when people are worried, especially when a crowd of ravenous campers have eaten only sandwiches and cake (and the odd ice cream) since breakfast. While Liz and the girls set about making the evening meal – a real mouth-waterer, with hotted-up steak and kidney puddings, and lashings of peas and gravy – Steve and the boys vanished in search of the wanderer.

'He'll be back as soon as he smells a good dinner cooking,' Wendy said hopefully. But Liz privately wondered whether Joe had moved on again, afraid that his hiding-place had been discovered.

The meal was almost ready before the boys began to drift back in ones and twos, tired and hungry. All had drawn blanks. In the end, Steve returned, disappointed as he scanned the faces of the other searchers.

'Not a sign of him anywhere,' said Steve wearily, sinking down on a camp stool. 'Anyone else see anything?' But even before he asked the question, he knew the answer. Steve glanced around the tent again. 'Where's Andrew?' he said.

'Not back yet,' said Karen. 'Come on – let's have our supper. I don't know about you lot, but I'm starving, and these puddings must be ready by now. I'm sure Joe will turn up in the morning.'

'I hope the police haven't found him,' said Neil. At that moment, the tent flap lifted, and Andrew came into the kitchen, excited and breathless. He threw a packet on to the table, narrowly missing a steaming steak and kidney pudding which had just been turned out on to a plate.

'Joe's sandwiches,' he said triumphantly. 'Only half of them eaten. Found 'em on the beach. Something must have disturbed Joe in the middle of his meal – there are footprints all over the place! It looks as though Joe went down to the rocks by the point.'

Neil jumped up suddenly, sending a tin plate crashing to the ground. 'Come on everybody,' he yelled. 'To the rescue!'

There was instant pandemonium as everyone tried to get up from the long table at once. The narrow bench tipped, and James, who had been sitting at the end, slid to the ground in a heap.

Steve brought the flat of his hand down on the table with a loud 'thwack!' There was a startled silence.

'Nobody goes out looking for Joe tonight!' he said, firmly. There was a chorus of mutinous disagreement.

'Oh, but Steve ...!'

'He might be in danger ...'

'How do you know that ...'

'Be quiet!' Steve ordered, authority in his voice. 'We have to do this thing logically!' His wife caught his eye, and smiled. 'First of all, how long will the light last tonight? About half an hour – an hour at the very most. Nobody is going to play mountain goat over cliffs and rocks in the dark. Remember what happened to Joe on those same rocks!'

The children had to admit that Steve was right – as usual.

'Tomorrow, we'll organize proper search parties to look for Joe, first thing after breakfast, if he hasn't turned up by then.'

'Good – no washing-up,' put in Peter, and Steve frowned at the interruption.

'Liz is driving the minibus out to Heystock tomorrow to find Joe's Mum and Dad, and bring them down here,' he went on.

There were immediate cheers which died quickly away as Steve added, 'So hurry up and finish your meal and get off to bed, the lot of you. We've an early start in the morning.'

*　　　*　　　*

If the night had been a long one for Joe, locked in his cold, dark outhouse, it seemed almost as long to Steve and Liz, more concerned about Joe than they cared to admit. A very early and rather silent breakfast was eaten and, as Peter had guessed, washing-up was left until later. He was not joking about it any more – things were much too serious. Though washing-up was put off, prayers were not, and Joe would have been amazed and pleased to hear the way his new friends prayed for him.

Steve divided the whole area into sections, and organized the searchers into groups of two or three. Each was given a particular area to go through thoroughly. The capable Ian, with two of the older girls, was directed to stay in the camp to look after Joe if he should come back, or be brought back injured. Liz had already left in the minibus for Joe's home, and the others were all itching to be off, too.

'Right then,' said Steve, finally. 'Everybody know exactly what they're doing?'

'Yes – but where will you be if any of us find him?' asked Wendy, sensibly.

'Good question,' said Steve. 'I'll have a look for him myself but I shan't be far away. If Joe's found, bring him straight back to camp.' He took off the shiny whistle which hung on a red cord around his neck, and handed it to Ian. 'Three long blasts on the whistle mean that Joe's found, or that there's some definite news of him. Wherever I am I'll hear it and come running. Whether he's found or not, we'll all re-assemble here at –' he glanced at his watch, 'ten o'clock. Off you go, then.'

Within a minute the searchers had gone, and Steve was standing in the circle of blue tents. He felt really uneasy about Joe – a nameless fear he could not explain. He gazed around him at the sea, the distant cliffs, the green hills, the wooded valley.

Somewhere out there was a frightened and desperate youngster doing all in his power to save the life of his dog. Who could tell what reckless thing Joe might do next? Steve sighed heavily. There was such an expanse of ground to cover – it seemed almost impossible that a handful of kids could find Joe.

'But you know where he is, Father,' he prayed. 'Take care of him, whatever he's doing, and bring him back to us safely.'

And suddenly confident, Steve squared his shoulders and set out.

CHAPTER 10

JOE MAKES
UP HIS MIND . . .

Though Steve had given clear instructions to each of the rescue parties, he had no real idea of the direction he himself would take. He climbed a stile and took the path through the woods – a pleasant enough walk at any other time. But Steve, on his grim search, had no time to spare for admiring the scenery.

As the trees thinned, and the woods gave way to grassy fields and hills, the pathway joined a wider dirt track which led away up the hill towards a farm on the cliff tops. Another narrow green lane wound back down through the fields to the sand dunes and the sea.

Steve was familiar with most of this area, but had never been along the farm track before. He turned in that direction now, walking purposefully, with a swinging stride. As he turned a corner, a small boy, streaked with dirt, tear-stained and rather smelly, cannoned into him, racing in the opposite direction. Steve held him fast by the shoulders.

'Joe!' he cried in relief, and Joe it was, though scarcely recognizable through the layers of dirt. 'Where in the world have you been? We've been awake half the night wondering where you could possibly be, and all the gang are out now, hunting for you!'

Joe could hardly believe that it really was Steve. He clutched his friend's arm and began to drag him up the lane towards the farm.

'Oh, Steve!' he gasped. 'You've got to help me – that man's got a shotgun – he's going to kill Sheba! He locked me up in his shed all night, and ...'

'Hang on a minute, Joe! Slow down and tell me the whole story.'

'But there's no time,' pleaded Joe, desperately. 'Any minute now he's going to find out that I've escaped, and he'll shoot her, I know he will! You have to come with me and stop him.'

Steve tried to calm the trembling boy. 'Joe, listen to me,' he said. 'There's only one way to tackle this thing, and that's the *right* way. I don't know who this man is who's threatening to shoot Sheba, but I do know that if he did that, he'd be in very serious trouble with the police. The police are the people to deal with this man.'

'No,' said Joe.

Steve looked into the boy's eyes. 'Look, Joe,' he said. 'I know you want to keep as far away as possible from the police right now, but...' Joe looked away at once, and shrugged Steve's hand off his shoulder.

'You have to level with me, Joe,' Steve said. 'I know all about it – their side of the story, anyway – we heard it on the radio. Now I want to know your side too. I'll do everything I can to help you. I can imagine something of what it's like for you, trying to protect Sheba when everything seems against you.'

Joe shook his head fiercely. 'No, you can't,' he said. 'Nobody could possibly know. I've had her ever since she was a puppy, and now they want to have her destroyed. You don't know what it's like at all!'

Steve looked thoughtful. 'Maybe I don't, Joe,' he said, wisely. He put his arm around Joe's shoulders. 'But I know someone who does know. God knows exactly what you feel like, and he may be the only one who can help you. But God really does answer prayer – we can ask him together to show us what to do.'

Joe suddenly remembered the prayer that God had already answered when he was locked up in the outhouse, and for the first time he dared to begin to hope.

'You mean that God can save Sheba?' he said.

Steve took a deep breath. This was where his own faith stood or fell. Joe was depending on him. Yet he and Liz had stuck their necks out and decided to trust God for that very thing.

'Yes – I mean just that, Joe,' he said, confidently.

'How do you know?' asked Joe, scowling.

'That's an easy one to answer,' said Steve. 'I know it because he's done so many things for me before. A long time ago, my life was one great mix-up, a bit like yours is right now. I was just like most other guys, looking for kicks – but only getting the knocks. It wasn't till I turned over my life to Jesus Christ – cheating, lying, rebelling – the lot – that I found out that God is still in business. He took hold of me and turned me right around. He gave me a life that's really worth living.'

Joe looked at the ground and shuffled his feet. For once he had nothing to say.

'Look here, Joe,' said Steve. 'There's more to this thing than saving Sheba. That's part of it, yes. But what about the other things? All the lies, the stealing – you know it all as well as I do. God wants to change all that. What about giving him a chance, Joe?'

Taken unawares, Joe suddenly saw himself with

new eyes. The things he'd pinched, the pack of lies he had told, the way he had treated his parents. A moment of guilt added to his misery. He shut it out.

'But what about Sheba?' he cried, furiously. Angry with himself, he took it out on Steve. 'That farmer might be loading his gun at this very minute! If God can really save Sheba, why can't he do it now?' He tugged at the sleeve of Steve's jersey. 'Come back to the farm with me – just talk to that man. Make him set Sheba free!'

Steve shook his head. 'That's not the right way to do it, Joe – I know it's not,' said Steve firmly. 'Let's find the nearest house and get someone to ring for the police. Come on – we'll go right now, as fast as we can.'

Joe rudely turned his back on Steve. 'The police will have her killed, even if the farmer doesn't!' he shouted. With a choke in his voice, he added, 'A fine friend you are – you won't help my dog. You don't care.' Joe began to walk down the hill.

'Joe! Joe, listen!' Steve shouted. 'Come back. Don't be a donkey!'

Joe began to run. 'If you won't help me, I'll find someone else who will!' he yelled defiantly over his shoulder. 'I hate you!'

Steve went after him, but Joe had a good start. He put on speed, and turned along the lane which led down through the sand dunes to the sea. Joe ran well, his bad ankle forgotten. The narrow lane ended in a stile, and he was over this in an instant. A twisty little path led through the sand dunes. Through the dunes and across the sand Joe raced, with Steve in close pursuit.

It was difficult, running across the soft deep sand, and Joe found himself slipping and floundering at every step. It was almost as bad as trying to run through fallen snow in winter time. Then his flying feet faltered for a second or two as he looked down the beach towards the headland and realized what a mistake he had made.

He should have turned the other way! His escape was already cut off by the sea. Further along, where the cliffs and rocks jutted out, the incoming tide was already deep. Steve was right behind him, gaining on him. He was losing valuable seconds. Which way could he turn?

An idea swiftly forming in his mind, Joe glanced quickly above him to the cliff face. Yes, it was not too high just here, and there were plenty of hand- and footholds and small ledges.

His mind made up, Joe quickly began to climb. He had been right – this was very easy going. His questing fingers found a wide scar in the rock, and Joe wedged his right foot above a little overhang. Then a good ledge helped him on. He was soon far above the beach.

'Joe!' Steve called from below. 'Come on down! Why are you running away? Just come down and let's talk.'

Joe couldn't have told anyone why he was running away. Had he been asked to explain, he would have been puzzled to know what to say. The most important thing, it seemed to him, was to give Steve the slip. He must get away by himself, somewhere he could think.

At that moment, he felt that he hated Steve. How could he save Sheba without Steve's help? But all *he* wanted to do was ring for the police! Black despair settled on Joe's heart. He rested for a minute to catch his breath, his cheek against the cold hard stone, then began to climb again.

Steve hesitated, then began to climb after him. 'Come down, Joe!' he shouted again.

'Leave me alone!' Joe shouted from above him.

'Go away and leave me alone.'

Joe was nearing the top of the cliff. Here and there, small bushes and shrubs had found enough earth to put down roots, and they helped him on. Yet this was also the most dangerous part of his climb. The old and weathered rocks had cracked and broken. More than once Joe's foot had slipped as loosened stones and earth had given way and gone rattling to the bottom.

Steve, taller and stronger than Joe, was making fast progress, and Joe, glancing below, saw that he was catching up. Quick, quick, he must get to the top, where he could run again. Here was another difficult bit – no firm grip for Joe's feet. He got his left toe well into a crack, reached out with his right hand and grasped the woody stem of a bush. But as he shifted his weight, he felt the roots loosen and give way. He made a grab for an overhang of rock, and his toe slipped.

For one awful minute, Joe was sure he was going to fall. But his handhold held firm, while his feet scrabbled to get a grip of solid rock. His right foot found a narrow ledge. But as Joe tested his weight on it, a sizeable chunk of rock came loose and fell away.

'Joe!' A single cry came from Steve, who was right below him. The rock struck a ledge then fell again, catching Steve heavily on the temple. Half-stunned by the blow, Steve lost his grip and dropped like a stone to the foot of the cliff, where he lay without moving.

With hammering heart, his fingers almost cracking under the strain of hanging on, Joe felt about for, and found, a firm foothold. He began to come back down the cliff carelessly, hurriedly, heedless now of his own safety.

What if Steve were dead? It would be *his* fault!

He jumped the last few feet, landing heavily beside Steve.

He was still breathing – Joe could see that – but lying so white and still! What could he do? Joe looked wildly about him. Steve had said that everyone else was out right now, looking for him. Surely some of the campers would be around? But the beach was deserted, and Joe felt an unreasonable anger. Why were people never around when you wanted them?

He stripped off his jersey and stuffed it under Steve's head. Now what? He had to get help for Steve from somewhere. Joe wasn't sure how badly he was hurt. But he'd need hospital treatment as quickly as possible. And he, Joe, was the only one who could help. Yet if he got involved with ambulance men and police, answering questions and making explanations, then he could say goodbye to any chance of saving Sheba.

Not according to Steve, though. Steve had been so sure that God could help him. But for the life of him, Joe couldn't see how he was going to do it. What was it that Steve had said? God really does answer prayer, and he's still in the business of solving problems, even today. Could God solve this one?

Joe hesitated no longer. 'God,' he said. 'I'm turning this problem over to you. I'm going to get help for Steve. But even if I have to talk to the police, please save Sheba somehow.'

The decision was made, and Joe felt a lot better. Now, where were the nearest houses? Surely one of them would have a 'phone. Then Joe remembered the smoke he had seen across the hills, that first day. He turned briefly again to the unconscious Steve.

'Hang on there,' he whispered, as if Steve could hear him. 'I'm going for help.' And Joe was off again, running like the wind.

CHAPTER 11

... AND FINDS OUT
FOR HIMSELF

The hospital was full of busy, bustling people, all of whom were too preoccupied here, in Casualty, to pay much attention to one small boy.

'Wait there,' they had told Joe, and left him perched forlornly on the edge of a chair, as they hurried Steve away on a trolley to the X-Ray department – and there he had waited. And waited.

At first, he had been glad enough to sit still for a while, bone-weary after his race to a 'phone, the tense minutes of waiting followed by the swift, anxious drive to the hospital with Steve, still white-lipped and unmoving. All this on top of his cold, sleepless night in the outhouse, his running away from Steve, and his reckless climbing of the cliff. No wonder Joe was worn out. He settled back on his chair and let himself relax. But as time went on he began to ask himself if he had been forgotten.

More than once it had crossed Joe's mind to slip away quietly, before he was recognized. But he badly wanted to know if Steve was going to be all right. Besides, what could he do if he did leave the hospital? Alone, he had no chance of saving Sheba's life. She could be dead already – unless God really was going to answer his prayer.

Joe waited on for what seemed like a very long time. A boy with a bad cut on his chin was taken to

84

have stitches put in. A man with his leg in a plaster was helped painfully to the door. A very small girl, clutching a threadbare teddy, and sucking her thumb, was brought in and carried away to the X-Ray room. Nobody seemed to notice Joe at all.

At last, he could stand it no longer. Slipping from his seat, he crossed the waiting-room to a desk where a young receptionist in a white overall was busily writing in a big book. She looked at Joe over her spectacles and gave him a quick smile.

'What can I do for you?' she said, then added cheerfully, 'You don't look very ill to me – though you could do with a bath.'

'It's not me, it's my friend ...' began Joe. The girl's telephone rang, and Joe had to waste more minutes, listening to her side of the conversation. His eyes roamed the room without interest, then focused on a newspaper lying to one side of the desk. It was upside down, but that picture looked awfully like ... it was, surely – himself with Sheba. Those pictures Dad had taken in the last holidays, at Bournemouth ... The girl saw him looking, and her eyes travelled from Joe's face to the picture, and back again.

'Yes, yes,' she said into the telephone. 'Look, something urgent just came up. I'll have to let you know about those admissions later. I'll ring you back.' She put the 'phone down like someone in a dream. 'Is your name Joe?' she said.

Here it comes, thought Joe. He couldn't avoid answering questions now.

'Yes,' he said.

The girl pushed the newspaper towards him.

'Have you seen this?' she asked him.

Joe shook his head, and turned the paper the right way up. With disbelieving eyes, Joe read the headline below the photograph: '"Killer Dog"

proved innocent – Come home, Joe, pleads mother.'
The small print went on to tell how Mr Benson, the
farmer had had more sheep attacked just the night
before. He and his men had hunted for, and shot,
the killer dog, which had been a red setter, very like
Sheba.

There was more, but Joe stared at the words,
suddenly unable to read on. Unexpectedly, his
throat tightened and he felt a sudden surge of happy
relief. God really *was* sorting things out! It was all
over. He and Sheba could go home. He could go
back to normal life again. He would be able to swim
for the school after all. The nightmare was ended.

But was it? A cold hand clutched at Joe's heart
again as he remembered that Sheba was still a
prisoner with that awful farmer. For all he knew, she
might be already dead! Surely, though, God
wouldn't let her be killed now, after all this? He
turned swiftly to the girl behind the desk, who was
using the telephone again.

'Will you please 'phone the police, and ask them
to come?' he said. 'It's terribly urgent.'

The girl nodded, then covered the mouthpiece
with her hand.

'I'm speaking to them right now,' she whispered.
'Don't you worry about it!' She took her hand away.

'Yes,' she said into the telephone, 'he's here
now, in the hospital … no, there's nothing wrong
with him – at least I don't think so … No, not the
dog, just Joe … Right. Fine. I'll keep him here with
me until you arrive.' She put down the receiver and
beamed at Joe.

'They'll be here in ten minutes,' she told him.

The Police Station could not have been far away.
In much less than ten minutes, two burly,
uniformed officers entered the waiting-room. Joe
could never have imagined, over the past few days

spent in desperate hiding, that he would be so very glad to see them. They knew Joe immediately, and strode across to the reception desk.

'Your parents'll certainly be glad to see you again, young man!' boomed one of them – the taller of the two. 'Been creating quite a stir, you have!'

The other one turned to the receptionist.

'How did he come to be here?' he asked. She spread out her hands and shrugged her shoulders.

'I just looked up, and there he was!' she said. 'I'm as mystified as you are.'

'I came with Steve in the ambulance,' Joe told them. 'He fell off a cliff, and I had to get help for him.'

'Who's Steve?' the policeman asked. But Joe went on without stopping.

'... But it's Sheba who needs help now,' he was saying. 'This farmer has her locked up – he says he's going to shoot her. He locked me up in his shed all night, but I got out with an axe ...'

'An *axe* you say? You've been smashing up people's property ...'

'I'll pay for the damage –' cried Joe impatiently, '– but you don't understand. He's going to kill my dog, he thinks she's a sheep killer, and she's not. He has a shotgun!'

The police officers were listening now with serious faces.

'Come on, son,' the big one said. 'We'll go and talk to this farmer. Where did you say he lives?'

'But first I have to know if Steve's going to be all right,' Joe protested. 'I can't go anywhere until I find out – you see, it was my fault that he fell. He was coming after me.'

'Who *is* this Steve?' the policeman asked again.

'He's in charge of a camp near the place where I've been staying. Oh – and the kids and Liz don't know what's happened to him! Steve saved my life when I was trapped by the tide. He's a friend.'

A look passed between the two officers.

'No,' said Joe hurriedly. 'It's not like that. He didn't know who I was until last night. I ran away from him when he wanted to tell the police about the farmer locking Sheba up.'

The tall officer turned to the receptionist. 'Can we find out about this young man?' he asked her.

She nodded. 'What's his other name?' She picked up the 'phone again.

'I don't know,' Joe said.

It did not seem to matter. She found out all Joe wanted to know straight away. She gave him a smile.

'Your friend has a broken leg, mild concussion, bruises, and cuts to the side of his head,' she said.

'That was the rock that fell on him,' said Joe, remembering the awful moment.

'Anyway,' she went on, 'he's going to be as good as new in no time – and the nurse said he sent you a funny message.' She looked puzzled. 'He said "remind Joe that God's still in business". It was something like that, anyway. Does that make sense to you?'

Joe nodded. 'It makes sense,' he said.

*　　　*　　　*

Joe had been sitting in the waiting-room for a very long time, with nothing happening at all. Now, suddenly things began to happen so rapidly that Joe could hardly keep up. He was whisked away in a fast police car. Radio messages were sent out, about getting in touch with Joe's parents, and about the others, alone at the camp, wondering where Steve could be.

'They'll have someone down there to keep an eye on them in two shakes,' one of the officers told Joe, who had been worrying about his friends. Joe's heart felt a little lighter. One by one, his worries were being taken care of. Now, if only they were in time to save Sheba, he would be perfectly happy.

The police car swung at last into the dirt track which led up to the farm. Joe pointed it out to them thankfully. The driver turned at speed through the still open gates and into the muddy farmyard. Both officers got out of the car. The big one turned and poked his head back inside.

'Best stay put, young Joe,' he said. 'We don't want you getting into any more trouble!' He slammed the car door and the two big men strode to the front door of the farmhouse and knocked loudly.

At that moment, from the back of the house, came the sudden, loud report of a shotgun. Joe, his heart in his mouth, was out of the car in a trice. He tore around the side of the farmhouse, beating the two officers, who had further to run. Was Sheba already dead?

'Please, God. No!' he sobbed as he ran.

As he rounded the corner, Joe was in time to see the farmer take aim once more – and, yes! Sheba had somehow escaped and was running across the field, limping badly, but still alive! Joe hesitated only for a moment. Then he charged on towards the farmer. Could he get there in time? The next shot might be a better one, and the man was about to fire again.

Joe leaped suddenly forward, butting the man in the stomach, with a head like a bullet. The shot went wide, and the man doubled over, winded.

'Oof!' he gasped. 'You just wait! I'll make you pay for that!' But Joe had not stayed to hear his threats.

'Sheba!' he shouted, haring across the field. There was a glad, answering bark. On three legs, Sheba ran rather jerkily back, and the two rolled over on the ground together, both of them wild with joy.

By the time Joe got back to the house, fussing over Sheba's hurt paw (which turned out to be a mere graze), the farmer had been taken into custody and was sitting sullenly in the back of the patrol car.

But what was this? Another vehicle was pulling into the farmyard. A van ... no, a minibus! Liz was at the wheel, and ... yes, it was!

'Mum! Dad!' shouted Joe.

When the hugging and backslapping were over, of course Joe wanted to know how they happened to come along just at the right moment.

'Simple,' said Liz. 'I went off first thing this morning to fetch your Mum and Dad down here,' (this was news to Joe) 'and when we got back to the camp the place was full of policemen. Well, two or three of them anyway. They told us where to find you and, Bob's your uncle – here we are.'

'Did they tell you what happened to Steve?' said Joe, anxiously.

'Yes, they did – but they told me he was going to be all right, which is what matters most. I'm going straight to the hospital to see him now.'

'Can I come, too?' pleaded Joe.

'Oh, Joe,' his mother protested. 'You need a bath and a good meal, and a good long sleep too, by the look of you.'

'A bath, mostly,' said Joe's father, drily. 'He'll have to get the dirt off with a file.'

'I've got something special to tell him,' persisted Joe. He caught Liz's eye and smiled suddenly. 'It's terribly important.'

Liz looked at Joe's father and raised her

eyebrows enquiringly.

'Oh, all right,' he said, 'if it's so important. But make it snappy, or we'll have your mother after the pair of us!'

'It won't take a minute,' said Joe, happily.

*　　　*　　　*

'Ten minutes only, please,' warned a nurse in a crackly apron who showed Liz and Joe into Steve's room.

Steve, looking rather like an Indian rajah with his head swathed, turban-like, in bandages, was sitting up in bed and looking more cheerful than most people do when they have fallen off a cliff.

Joe felt completely tongue-tied at first, and couldn't think of anything to say. But Steve put him quite at ease by clapping him hard on the back and giving his shoulders a hefty squeeze.

'What did I tell you?' he said to Joe. 'I knew God could fix it for you! They told me all about it.'

'I'm sorry I ran away and made you fall, Steve,' faltered Joe. 'I must have been crazy. And I didn't mean it at all when I said I hated you. I don't know why I said it.'

'Don't think about it any more,' said Steve. 'It's OK, kid.' He pulled himself up into a more comfortable position, and Liz gave his pillows a shake, and tucked them behind him again.

'I still feel awful about it, though,' went on Joe. 'I keep thinking about Andrew and Neil and the others. They'll all have to pack up and go home, now they don't have you and Liz to look after them, and the holidays aren't over yet. And it's all my fault.'

Steve gave him a cheerful grin. 'You don't have to worry about that, either,' he told Joe. 'As soon as

Liz 'phoned through to let them know at the church, Gordon and Molly said straight away that they would take over from us. They're great. And they'll be at the camp by teatime today. Pity you can't be there with them.'

'I have to go home,' said Joe. 'But I'd like to see you all again, some time.'

'Of course you will,' said Liz.

'By the way, Joe,' Steve went on. 'About that farmer who shot at Sheba ... I've been hearing a lot about him from one of your police officers.'

'What about him?' asked Joe.

'Don't be too hard on him, Joe, that's all,' said Steve. Joe looked at him in surprise, and Steve explained. 'He's had it rather rough over the last few years. First of all he lost his wife, and then the farm began to go downhill. A couple of years ago, he lost a lot of sheep to a dog that had been running wild, and he was almost ruined. Apparently, the poor man needs more of our sympathy than blame – he's going to be well cared-for in hospital for a while.'

'Why don't we send him some magazines or something?' suggested Liz.

'I could take him a basket of strawberries from our garden,' said Joe. 'Dad won't mind – he grows lots, and they'll soon be ripe.'

'Good idea!' said Steve, very glad that Joe wasn't going to bear the man a grudge. Just then, the door opened and the nurse popped her white-capped head inside.

'I think you should be going now,' she said. 'We don't want to over-tire the patient, do we?' She disappeared again.

'I'll pop in again at visiting time tonight,' said Liz. 'Come on, Joe, or we'll have that nurse in here again, on the warpath.'

'I'll ask my Dad if he'll run me down to see you again at the weekend,' said Joe. 'Thanks for everything.'

He went out after Liz, and the door swung to behind them. Immediately, it opened again, and Joe's head appeared once more.

'Thanks for your message,' he said, hurriedly. 'I found out for myself that God's still in business – I'm turning *my* life over to him!'

Steve lay back on his pillows. He was satisfied. The door closed again, and this time it stayed shut.